Sloan Surprised Her By Sliding His Hands Into Her Hair And Covering Her Lips With His Own.

Ziara's eyes slid shut as the explosion of sensation overwhelmed her and reason and logic disappeared. He could do what he wanted with her.

Just don't stop touching me.

Never one to do things by half measures, Sloan deepened the kiss, igniting a flash of longing through her body. Only after the last of her intelligence had leaked from her brain did he pull back a fraction. His hands remained anchored in her hair, his minty breath fanning across her face.

Forcing her heavy lids upward, her eyes met his. "What was that for?" she asked, embarrassed by the husky whisper of her voice.

His hands tightened against her head for a moment as if to draw her forward for another kiss, but instead he spoke. "For keeping my secrets."

Dear Reader,

I'm sure you've noticed our exciting new look! Harlequin Desire novels will now feature a brand-new cover design, one that perfectly captures the dramatic and sensual stories you love.

Nothing else about the Harlequin Desire books has changed. Inside our pages, you'll still find wealthy alpha heroes caught in unforgettable stories of scandal, secrets and seduction.

Don't miss any of this month's sizzling reads....

CANYON by Brenda Jackson
(The Westmorelands)

DEEP IN A TEXAN'S HEART by Sara Orwig
(Texas Cattleman's Club)

THE BABY DEAL by Kat Cantrell
(Billionaires & Babies)

WRONG MAN, RIGHT KISS by Red Garnier

HIS INSTANT HEIR by Katherine Garbera
(Baby Business)

HIS BY DESIGN by Dani Wade

I hope you're as pleased with our new look as we are. Drop by www.Harlequin.com or use the hash tag #harlequindesire on Twitter to let us know what you think.

Stacy Boyd

Senior Editor

Harlequin Desire

DANI WADE

—

HIS BY DESIGN

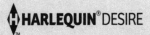

HARLEQUIN®DESIRE

To my incredible husband,
who has encouraged me every step on this journey.
You are the light when I am lost in darkness…
and a part of every hero I write.

Recycling programs
for this product may
not exist in your area.

ISBN-13: 978-0-373-73263-0

HIS BY DESIGN

Copyright © 2013 by Katherine Worsham

Printed in U.S.A.

www.Harlequin.com

DANI WADE

astonished her local librarians as a teenager when she carried home ten books every week—and actually read them all. Now she writes her own characters, who clamor for attention in the midst of the chaos that is her life. Residing in the Southern U.S. with a husband, two kids, two dogs and one grumpy cat, she stays busy until she can closet herself away with her characters once more.

Dear Reader,

I'm both excited and nervous to bring you my debut Harlequin Desire, *His by Design,* featuring a couple I've been in love with for a long time. You see, I'm fascinated by characters with hidden depths. Ziara Divan is a particular favorite, because I had the privilege of watching her pull herself out of her unfortunate childhood with hard work and dedication. She just needs someone to loosen her up a little, and Sloan Creighton is definitely the man for the job. Add in wedding dresses, hot Southern nights and a feuding family, then Ziara signed on for more than she anticipated.

I'm looking forward to hearing from my readers (I can't believe I can actually say that!). Please visit my website at www.daniwade.com or friend me on Facebook or follow me on Twitter to let me know if you enjoyed Ziara and Sloan's romance!

Dani

One

This was not how her morning was supposed to play out.

Ziara Divan rushed down the hallway of Eternity Designs, her brain pounding with the knowledge that she was late. Her cheeks burned as a result of her jog from the parking garage in workday pumps, and her suit skirt rode up the panty hose strangling her legs.

She threw her purse under her desk and grabbed her tablet from the drawer, turning it on as she continued down the hall with more speed than decorum. Rounding the corner into Vivian Creighton's outer office, Ziara ground to a halt. Vivian's assistant's desk was empty.

Breathe, Ziara. Pull yourself together.

She straightened her clothes in an attempt to regain her prized professional facade. But the agitated urgency to move, to get into the office quickly, still pounded in her chest. She wasn't perfect, but she made sure she came pretty dang close as an executive assistant in training, no matter how many minutes she spent stuck on a backed-up Georgia interstate.

As she struggled to regulate her breathing, Ziara heard

voices from beyond the door to the inner sanctum. At first, she couldn't grasp the idea that someone was yelling, because this was Vivian's office. Vivian didn't yell. It went totally against the traditional Southern rules of behavior for all ladies. But Vivian's voice was definitely raised. Ziara inched closer.

The other voice was male, deep. *Oh no.*

"...will not let you ruin my father's company..."

Sloan Creighton. Vivian's stepson. He came into the office rarely, but when he did he brought a tornadic level of energy and caused an unwanted tingle of awareness at the base of Ziara's spine. Though she studiously avoided him on his rare visits, he always seemed to find her. And flirt with her. And just generally turn her sense of professionalism upside down. The best reason to avoid him.

Vivian's own voice was muffled, but parts of Sloan's words came through the solid wood.

"...our biggest buyer rejected all the designs..."

Ziara's heart sank, threatening to drop out of her chest. Her knees went weak enough to force her to grab the frame of the door.

Ziara had suspected that last week's meeting with their largest retail account hadn't gone as planned, but the few who had attended were keeping quiet. Losing that buyer could mean ruin for Eternity Designs, something Ziara didn't want to see happen. She loved her job; this place, these people had also provided the stability and acceptance that had been lacking her entire life.

"...you have no choice..."

And neither did Ziara. She had to go through that door. Vivian had said to be in her office at eight sharp; it was now 8:17 a.m. But the thought of Sloan and the way his cool, effortless good looks and flirty attitude affected her body and her psyche made her want to return to the crowded freeway.

But backing down wasn't an option. With a deep breath to fortify herself, she headed through the doorway.

Sloan stood tall over Vivian, his voice ringing clear in the room. "I *will* have more voice in Eternity Designs, starting now. I'll need the next three months. If my fall line is a hit with our buyers, you will sign over enough of your shares for me to own fifty-five percent…and relinquish complete creative control. To. Me."

Ziara paused just inside the door, her mind absorbing those incredible words, while Sloan and Vivian glared at each other across Vivian's desk. For a moment Ziara's panic overrode everything, even the tempting sight of Sloan's strong shoulders and firm backside.

As the tension crept higher and higher, Ziara finally broke. Into the silence, she said, "Would you like me to come back, Vivian?"

Like pushing Play on a paused DVD, Vivian and Sloan both turned and looked in her direction. She met Vivian's eyes first, checking in with her boss and mentor. The narrowed glare and tight mouth signified a frustration that radiated like a cracked web through Vivian's normal composure. As if she realized how she must look, Vivian straightened, smoothing her elegant close-cropped curls into place. "Good morning, Ziara. Please sit."

"Now, Sloan," she said, turning her attention back to him. "Explain to me why I would ever agree to such ridiculous demands."

Sloan was too happy to comply. "Let me guess, commissions are down, creditors are closing accounts and you don't have a clue how to get yourself out of this situation." He straightened with confidence. "But I do."

"I'm sure I can find someone else to do the same."

"In enough time to make a difference? I don't think so."

She conceded to her stepson's ultimatum by leaning back in her chair, her composure shaken enough that she fiddled with the wedding band still gracing her left hand.

At least she didn't seem to notice—or care—that Ziara was late. Sloan, on the other hand, started cataloging everything about her. His gaze traveled down the length of her body to her toes, then back up with leisurely enjoyment.

Dragging her own composure around her like a cloak that

granted her invisibility, Ziara walked with measured steps across the carpeting to a chair beside Vivian's desk. A glance from under her lashes caught Sloan's interested stare zeroing in on the V of her suit jacket, where the modest edge of a lacy camisole peaked into view. With a great struggle, she forced herself not to adjust, to hold still while his eyes wandered back up to her vulnerable neck. The knowing smirk on his contoured lips sparked arousal beneath her irritation, confusing her further.

Damn man. She could see why Vivian found him so infuriating—professional behavior seemed to be a foreign concept to him. She'd seen the spark of interest before, though never quite this blatantly. Of course, his simple presence had always created an uncomfortable heat in her core that prompted her to keep any previous meetings as short and far apart as possible.

If she'd simply passed him on the street, Ziara would never have suspected him of the professional dedication he was displaying now. His collar-length, sun-streaked hair and the slight crook of his previously broken nose said "surfer boy" more than it did "hard-hitting negotiator." But the perfectly tailored dress shirt and pants, paired with his take-no-prisoners attitude, demonstrated the real man inside. His electric-blue eyes confirmed her suspicions that his core was pure steel.

She was thankful when he turned back to his stepmother. "This is my father's legacy we're talking about, Vivian. I save other people's businesses every day. Resurrecting Eternity Designs is right up my alley," he said.

"Yes," Vivian said, letting the word draw out. "Your…fix-it-up business."

"You could call it that. I call it the very lucrative process of taking failing companies and turning them into profit-making machines. Too bad you didn't get in touch with me sooner, but then you'd have to admit that you screwed up."

The slap of Vivian's hand on her desk made Ziara jump. She watched her with wide eyes, shocked by the venom scarring Vivian's normally genteel facade.

"Your father didn't trust you to take care of his legacy enough to leave it all to you. Why should I?"

Sloan stalked back and rested his hands on the desk, so he could loom over his stepmother. "And whose fault was that? Who slipped poisonous thoughts into his mind from day one, turning him against me so he could be yours and yours alone? Hell, Vivian, if I didn't know better, I'd think you set his whole will up. You're the one who made him insist I go for my MBA instead of continuing to pursue my own plans of fashion design, aren't you?"

"I don't know what you're talking about."

"Of course you do. After all, going from Daddy's assistant to his wife meant you got to control his entire life and not just his business, didn't it?"

Oh. Dear. Ziara's lungs shut down, trapping the air inside. Vivian's early involvement with Eternity Designs had never been explicitly discussed. Ziara had simply assumed she'd started working with the company sometime after she'd married Mr. Creighton.

The knowledge left Ziara reeling. How many times had Vivian admonished her that only tramps got involved with their coworkers? Ever since her childhood, when Ziara had been bullied because of her mother's lack of morals, she'd avoided anything that would suggest she was the same. Vivian's lessons had simply reinforced Ziara's focus on professionalism and the building of a flawless reputation.

Vivian's hand shook as she pointed at her stepson. "Don't talk to me that way, Sloan. It's disrespectful. Your father would never approve of your tone."

Sloan leaned in, hard. "Well, he's not here to reprimand me. If you wanted my respect, you should have tried earning it a long time ago. Now it's too late."

"It's never too late to expect you to be a gentleman. But we just couldn't get those lessons to stick."

Sloan laughed, collapsing into the chair as his body shook with a tainted kind of humor. Ziara felt like she was watching a tennis match. Sloan clearly thought he was the winner.

Vivian conceded with less graciousness than Ziara had ever seen her display, but then again, she'd learned quite a few new things about her mentor in the past ten minutes. Vivian hadn't always been a lady. Disbelief still ricocheted throughout Ziara like the ball inside a pinball machine.

"Fine, Sloan. Do whatever it is you do," Vivian forced out through clenched teeth.

"I'll have that in writing, I think," Sloan said.

"As demanding as you are, I'm amazed anyone will work with you."

"Oh, I'll manage," he said with a cocky quirk of his shapely lips.

"Not alone, you won't. The last thing I need is you wandering around unattended."

"Aw, Vivian. I didn't know you cared. Oh wait, you don't," Sloan said with saccharin sweetness.

"I care about Eternity Designs," she said.

His gaze scanned Vivian's face as if to determine the catch. "Anyone you saddle me with better know what they're doing and how to take orders."

"Oh, I have no doubt she'll work like a charm…and be able to keep you in line."

Ziara's heart picked up speed when Vivian's elegant, bejeweled fingers waved in her direction. *No. No, no, no.* The effort to hide her sudden panic and appear in control might just give her a heart attack.

Vivian's voice trickled through her consciousness, breaking her inward focus. "Your history with assistants is well-known, Sloan. They crawl all over you like bees in honey. That won't be an issue with Ziara. I've trained her well. She knows more about how we conduct business here than anyone except my own assistant. And her behavior is impeccable—unlike yours."

What was she—a slave girl at auction? *Would the buyer prefer pretty and pliable or plain but talented?* Though dependable was exactly the look she was going for, the thought still disconcerted her.

"Well, Vivian, isn't that thoughtful of you?" he said.

Ziara glanced up to find Sloan's gaze directed her way. His earlier anger had turned his bright blue eyes icily sharp, his body rigid, his jaw tight. But now he eased back in a chair, propping his elbows on the arms. His fingers absently stroked the upper ridge of his lip, drawing her attention to the sensuous curve of his mouth. His turbulent look suddenly softened like ice thawing beneath a heat lamp.

Her emotions seesawed as his gaze traveled south, visually caressing the extra length of leg exposed by her hasty drop into her chair. She could almost feel his touch sliding along the edge of her skirt, tickling the sensitive skin on the backs of her legs.

Bit by bit, Ziara used up her willpower forcing herself to sit impassively. The twitch of her thighs urged her to shift her feet, but she resisted. That would tell him just how much he affected her. Tightening her muscles, she tried to crack down on the spreading fire, to no avail. Ignoring physical desire had never been a problem before him.

Her new boss.

Her soothingly subtle gray business suit, so comfortable in the luxurious air-conditioning only moments ago, now felt heavy, itchy. Her nipples peaked against their confinement. She felt that he peered through her professional armor to the woman she kept hidden deep inside.

How could a simple look make her so aware, too aware? As if she lacked something only he could provide.

As casually as possible, she adjusted her position and her skirt, covering her legs down past her knees.

Knowledge leaked into his eyes, as well as smug satisfaction. *He did that on purpose.* Feeling a need to defend herself, she met him with a flick of her lashes. Slowly she lifted her left brow.

He grinned, not at all intimidated by her challenge. "Be in my office and ready to work first thing tomorrow morning."

She could handle his antagonistic, dismissive tone; she welcomed it to counteract her strange reaction to him. Unlike efficient orders and professional expectations, the sensations created with that hot, hard stare set her nerves on edge.

But she could handle it. She'd pulled herself up from a sludge-pile existence and become a woman with goals and dreams and skills. She could control herself for the three months it would take to get Eternity Designs back in the spotlight and earn her stripes as an executive assistant. But how was she going to control him?

Ziara. Her classic beauty and calm demeanor distracted Sloan from Vivian's condescension. Staring his new assistant down made him hotter than he'd been in a long time. Vivian's insistence that Ziara wouldn't follow the path of his previous assistants didn't worry him. As annoying as it had been to replace three employees in less than two years because they insisted they were *in love* with him, he might have to pursue this woman. Her pretend lack of interest challenged him, but turning Ziara's head could provide plenty of ammunition in his war with Vivian.

How ironic that the very thing he'd avoided in his professional life—intimate involvement with an employee—could give him a leg up in this situation. It felt wrong even thinking that way, but winning her loyalty could give him the freedom to do whatever he wanted without Vivian's interference. He needed every advantage to fight against Vivian. His stepmother was totally immune to his charm, which drew cheeky toddlers, blue-haired dames and women of every age in between. If Vivian had been a typical trophy wife, at least Sloan could have fallen back on his practiced grin and genuine appreciation of the female species, but, instead, dear old Dad had the foresight to marry a savvy woman. One steeped in Southern tradition and brimming with a Southern belle's ingenuity to survive. Too bad her temperament had always favored Scarlett's machinations as opposed to Melanie's sweetness.

She viewed his father's memory and Eternity Designs as hers; Sloan was a threat to her reign as queen. His frustration had been building over this situation for years and he let it out for once.

"We need to shake things up," he said. "We can't afford to

lose our biggest account because we're afraid to break out of the mold. Reliance on tradition is getting you nowhere. Eternity Designs needs a modern edge, a new designer, a revamped portfolio. Pronto."

That was exactly what Vivian didn't want to hear. "Your father prided himself on the tradition inherent in this company and its designs," she said, elegantly restrained anger sharpening her tone. "This discussion demonstrates exactly why he chose me to continue the legacy of Eternity Designs."

Not you.

The wedding gown design firm had been in his family for three generations—if his current 40 percent share of it counted for anything. With Vivian, it didn't. But the words of the accountant told him now was the time to insist on the control she'd denied him for so long.

"The whole company will go under if something isn't done immediately."

"Sixty percent ownership doesn't mean you're God," he said, ignoring the burn of betrayal. "It's a good thing dear ol' Dad isn't alive to see how you've run it into the ground." Yep. Payback was a bitch.

A quick glance revealed Ziara stiffening, in surprise or defense he wasn't sure. If she knew what the posture did for her magnificent breasts, she'd hunch in on herself for eternity. He paced back and forth in front of Vivian's desk, arousal and frustration fueling his restlessness. The business expert in him was tired of talking.

The man in him begged for a totally different kind of action.

Watching Ziara's reactions to his and Vivian's little fight fascinated him more than he would have thought. Her exotic, raven-haired beauty brought to mind sensual, spice-scented nights. What would she look like with that thick bun let loose around her shoulders? With that suit jacket loosened up a few buttons? Seducing her out of her loyalty to Vivian was going to be such guilty fun.

He'd avoided getting involved with his employees like a contagious disease, to the point that he hadn't even had an assistant for six months. But his desperation called for outrageous actions—like storming into Vivian's office this morning. Finding out Ziara had given up company loyalty for carnal indulgence would probably mean a quick dismissal, but he couldn't let that stop him. For Ziara this was a job; she'd find another one soon enough.

For Sloan, Eternity Designs was a legacy.

Vivian's haughty belle persona reappeared. "You're awfully sure of yourself, Sloan. Overconfidence leads to nasty downfalls. Those unconventional methods of yours won't work in such a traditional company."

"Those unconventional methods are just what Eternity needs. Less tradition, not more." He turned to Ziara. Might as well put her to the test first thing. "What do you think? Is Eternity's current path leading to success?"

"I…I…" Her almond-shaped eyes flicked back and forth between him and her mentor, panic darkening their chocolate color. After a moment she said, "Our designers do beautiful work, enough to build a loyal following. Families come here generation after generation to commission their dresses. Our motto, our focus has built a legacy. I have no proof otherwise."

Test number one: fail.

Vivian echoed Ziara's words. "Eternity Designs is truly *where tradition and style forever align*."

Quoting the company's motto as a defense ramped up Sloan's anger. He needed to save this business. His father had worked hard to build it. He'd loved it just as Sloan did. Despite their differences at the time of his death, the 40 percent he'd gifted to Sloan in his will told him his father had wanted him to have some small part of his family's heritage. He had to believe that, had to believe Vivian hadn't poisoned every ounce of their father-son bond.

He glared at them both. "Maybe our motto needs to change."

Ziara held very still, the only movement the frantic pulse beating at the base of that silky throat. But Vivian sighed heavily, with a touch of drama. She would have called it flair. He knew he wouldn't like what came next.

"I've been thinking about options to get us through this little slump. I have a few friends who might know potential backers. That should tide us over until spring."

Shock immobilized Sloan for a moment. Then a sharp spike of panic sliced through the numbness. Then another…and another. "We're not letting an outsider buy into this company."

"I'll do what I have to in order to save Eternity."

"Except call in the one man whose skills would provide the lifeline? Did you honestly think I'd sit back, mouth shut, while you let Eternity go out of the family?" He straightened, the hardball negotiator stepping onto the court. "You know me better than that, Vivian."

With a blink, uncertainty leaked into Vivian's eyes. "I truly don't understand why you'd care."

He shook his head slowly, sorrow over the state of his relationship with his late father leaking underneath the anger. "That right there proves how little you know me…or knew my father. This place was his life—" in the end more than even his son "—I want nothing more than for his life's work to continue, to prove to his memory I'm more than you made me out to be. A hard worker, capable of contributing to the family dream, instead of a slacker who cares about nothing but myself. You're still looking at me as a grieving kid, Vivian. Not the man I've actually become, the man my father saw in me before he died."

But the tightening around her mouth told him she'd never see it that way. After years of convincing her husband that his only son was impulsive and undependable, repeatedly citing his teenage antics, his father had left *her* with the majority ownership of Eternity Designs. That's all she cared about.

"Sloan, I would prefer to keep this inside family lines, such as they are. So I'll stand by my word and give you a chance. But in the meantime, I'll be working on a backup plan."

It wasn't much of a compromise, as they went, but he'd take what he could get. He needed carte blanche over the fall line. Because if Vivian knew the plans gathering mass in his mind, she'd shut him down in a heartbeat.

Her mouth pulled into a strained smile. "Just don't go forgetting who is in charge around here."

"I won't. We'll pretend you're in charge while I become the linchpin holding everything together."

It was a low blow, but he was beyond caring. Vivian straightened, her shoulders squaring as the pinching around her mouth deepened. Then a calculating look slid across her face, warning him he was about to pay for his disrespect.

"I have a caveat of my own. If you should happen to walk away before the fall line is presented—" her tone said she could happily run him off with a shotgun "—then Eternity Designs will become solely mine."

Two

Nothing like a new challenge and a gorgeous woman to work with.

Sloan listened to Ziara's movements in the outer office as he sat at his desk. He'd wondered whether she'd postpone coming in until the last minute, but here she was thirty minutes early, moving into her new office.

Yesterday she'd both confounded and fascinated him. Her exotic, Indian beauty stirred many un-bosslike urges. Her attempts to keep that beauty under wraps teased his senses. Did she think pulling her luxurious dark hair tight into a bun and covering those shapely legs made her a better employee? It probably did in Vivian's eyes, but Sloan was a whole other matter.

Something she'd learn soon enough, and hopefully enjoy. Though he'd never seduced any of his employees—he spent more time running from than running after—he wasn't above using this mutual attraction as one more tool to secure control of Eternity Designs. He would need her help to understand how things worked around here, to facilitate his relationships with the other employees after being shut out in the cold since his father's death. If tempting her loyalty in his direction meant the reports to Vivian became fewer and further between, or even stopped, all the better.

Crossing the room with a heightened sense of anticipation, he eased through without alerting her to his entrance. She stood behind the desk, the chair pushed aside to give her room to reallocate her personal stuff. Her movements were elegant but efficient as she placed pens and papers in the desk drawers. Her careful concentration told him she had a precise way she wanted things and she'd find a way to create order in this new space.

He barely held back laughter as he sized her up. He was a red-blooded male and his body naturally heated despite her choice of clothes. She'd opted for a longer skirt and boxier jacket, as if that would hide the curvy shape of her hips and ass. But it was the scarf he found most amusing. From the back, he could see the curl of material around her neck. Did it merely cover her throat in the front, or had she gone all out to hide every single hint of bare skin, tucking the ends into her jacket?

Didn't she realize that *don't touch me* attitude set her up as his own personal challenge?

"Settling in okay?" he asked.

Her jerk of surprise should have made him feel guilty, but he suspected he had to sneak up on this one before she cut him off at the knees with her stern librarian attitude.

"Yes," she said. "I'm almost ready."

"No hurry," he murmured, tracking the glide of her fingers over a few pictures. No people that he could see, just atmospheric photographs of simple wooden bridges, each in a different season. She arranged them carefully along the top of the nearby shelf, then reached into the remaining cardboard box once more.

Pulling out an object wrapped in cotton batting, she uncovered it layer by layer. She steadily revealed a glass object inscribed with words that she rubbed over a few times with the wrapping.

Too quick for her to stop him, he lifted the object from her hands for a closer look. "What's this?" he asked.

"Be careful."

"Ziara, you wound me," he said with a cheesy helping of drama. "I promise not to drop it."

The cut-glass award was shaped in the outline of a flowing gown, inscribed with the date and Employee of the Year. Ziara Divan. "Employee of the Year, huh?"

"I've worked hard to get where I am."

"And where is that exactly?"

"If all goes well, I'll be promoted to Vivian's personal assistant when Abigail retires next spring."

"Wow, a full-fledged executive assistant at the tender age of—"

She drew a deep breath, as if he were a toddler trying her patience. "Twenty-seven."

"So young to be so buttoned-down." He aimed a pointed look at her scarf, which did indeed drape down to cover that delectable collarbone and upper chest.

"There are worse things to be."

"Like what?"

For a moment it looked like she would speak, but then those full lips pressed tight. Her hand extended, palm up, and her perfectly manicured fingertips curled in a *give it to me* gesture. "Behave, please."

He stepped closer, moving past her invisible *keep away* signs. "Let's get something straight here, Ziara. You're playing by my rules now. I'd imagine I have seriously different requirements for becoming *Employee of the Year.*"

She swallowed hard. "Excuse me?"

She reached for the award, moving her body even closer to him, and he used the opportunity to snag an edge of the scarf. Luckily for him, it was only loosely twisted and unraveled like a dream from around her neck and into his hands.

Award forgotten, her hands clamped to her bare neckline, then she glared at him. "What do you think you're doing?"

"A little employee training." He rubbed the material between his fingers but resisted the urge to lift it to his nose and find out if it smelled like her. Vanilla and cinnamon spice. "I'm not nearly as stuffy as Vivian. I don't run my office that way."

"Mr. Creighton—"

"Uh-uh. Sloan."

He was surprised she could talk through teeth that tightly clenched. "Sloan, your behavior is inappropriate in the extreme."

"Is it? Are you going to charge me with sexual harassment?"

That cool eyebrow lifted in condemnation. "If I have to."

Her response was so unexpected, he almost choked. Man, he sure enjoyed a woman with spice, but she didn't need to know that. Yet. "Oh, I don't think you will."

She opened her mouth, but he continued on. "I know Vivian gave you this job for a reason." He leaned even closer to her, watching her heartbeat speed up in the well of her collarbone. "And not just because you're organized and can turn in paperwork on time. After all, she knows something about assistants and their access to—how can I say this diplomatically—company secrets."

Not even an attempt at a response this time.

He pushed a little harder. "Isn't that right, Vivian's little spy?"

"That's insulting."

But she didn't look insulted. The waver of her gaze and uncertain look meant one thing: guilt. "There's no point in pretending, Ziara. Vivian put you here to keep an eye on me, and report back everything she needs—or doesn't need—to know. But that's okay."

Her eyes jerked back to his, widening to give him a great view of chocolate irises shot with gold sparks.

"Just remember," he said, "forewarned is forearmed."

For long seconds neither of them moved, gazes locked in either a worthy battle or forbidden attraction, he wasn't sure. All he felt was the blood pumping hard in his veins and an excitement he hadn't brought to a job in many, many years.

With shaking hands she finally pulled the award from his

grasp and turned to place it on the corner of her desk. Then, she pulled out a thick folder from a drawer of the filing cabinet. "Here is information on the current preparations for the fall line. I thought—"

He lifted the file from her unsteady hands, resentment that he had to rely on her for information mixing with the other emotions roiling through him. "What do we have here?"

She managed to maintain an outward calm. Almost. "Actually, I thought you might like me to familiarize myself with the project *you're here for*."

Her eyes begged, a moment of peace, but he wasn't in the mood for mercy. "Let's take this discussion into my office."

A spy, he'd said. She'd never really thought about it that way.

How had she been promoted from executive assistant in training to spy in one morning? Proving herself to Vivian had been a long-held goal, but doing it now could put her in a very awkward position.

One last glance at her Employee of the Year award stilled her spinning universe. Looking at it, her uneasiness and frustration melted away and her resolve strengthened.

This is what I want. I'm almost there. Becoming executive assistant to the CEO of a major design firm had been her goal from her first day at Eternity Designs. At twenty-seven, the finish line loomed much closer than she'd dared to hope, despite the lack of money for anything other than a trade school degree.

She'd grown up with nothing—no, less than nothing. Oh, they'd technically had enough to live on, but every spare cent had gone for slutty clothes and accessories for her mother to attract the newer, better sugar daddy around the corner.

She'd dreamed of escaping from the trash that still stained her heart into her own office situated right outside of her role model Vivian Creighton's. But would the price be worth this sacrifice?

Vivian and Sloan are playing a game and I'm stuck in the middle.

Ziara was smart enough to realize it. Her firm loyalty to

Vivian notwithstanding, her choices from here on out had to be dedicated to what was best for Eternity Designs. That was her only guarantee of keeping a clear conscience.

Vivian had given her a long lecture on all things Sloan yesterday afternoon. *He's not to be trusted. Why wouldn't his father have just given him the business if he wanted him to run it? He's up to something, I know it.* Ziara had questions of her own, concerns about a man who spent his life reviving companies but completely ignored his family heritage until it was almost too late. If Sloan truly sought to ruin the company, as Vivian had also suggested…well, she wasn't about to let him put anything over on her.

She'd just watch closely and learn to deal with him. She'd always been a stellar student. If she hesitated before crossing the threshold into his office, it didn't mean anything. Drawing in a deep breath, she straightened her shoulders. A little over three months and her training period would be complete. This was simply a small bump on a long road.

She pushed the dilemmas from her mind and entered the room.

Sloan had chosen a corner office at the opposite end of the building from Vivian's, his windows overlooking the sidewalk and shops that lined the streets in this part of town. Quaint, with a touch of subdued elegance, Ziara had always thought, and easily accessible through a MARTA stop only a few blocks away.

Instead of the soothing cream carpet prevalent in the rest of the offices, the flooring here had been replaced with dark wood planks. A desk just a shade or two darker dominated one corner, facing out so that Sloan could see the entire room, from the door to the floor-to-ceiling windows. He crossed the thick blue-and-burgundy rug to stand before them now, hands in his pockets, looking down from the fifth-story view.

For long moments he remained silhouetted against the lightened windows. His strong shoulders spoke of strength and shelter. The line tapered down to his waist, where his hands in his pockets drew the material of his dress pants across the high, firm cheeks of his backside.

Ziara shook her head slightly, grateful he couldn't see her. Being close to this overwhelmingly masculine presence on a daily basis had the potential to open up a whole host of dark desires she preferred to keep locked deep inside. Choosing a leather chair a safe distance away, she sat, primly crossing her legs at the ankles. She held herself rigid as she prepared to take notes, make phone calls, whatever he wanted of her.

"Did you know this was once my father's office?"

Surprise skittered through Ziara's controlled pose. "No," she murmured.

"I used to play right here on a rug while he worked," Sloan said. "I used to watch him stare out these same windows, while he worked out problems."

His voice was easy, soft with memory. He started to pace, firm steps along the length of the windows. Two glorious views. Candy for her sweet-starved eyes.

But warning lights started flashing through her brain as she thought about his words. She'd never had any type of loving parental relationships, and had cut all ties with her mother at the age of seventeen. But Sloan seemed to feel very passionately about his father, despite Vivian's insistence that Mr. Creighton had found his son a huge disappointment. Why had Sloan—

No. Thinking about Sloan's private life—his childhood, wishes, regrets—could not lead to anything good. Personalizing him outside of their business interactions would weaken her objectivity. She had to focus on work, not skipping through fantasyland.

After a minute or two, he clasped his hands behind his back, his long fingers tapping against his palms. "First things first," he murmured. "Where to start—"

"I've got a list here from Mrs. Creighton, and—"

His laughter echoed through the room, the sound truly amused rather than the nasty version she'd heard in Vivian's office. He paused in his imaginary trek to catch his breath and clutched his chest in mock astonishment. "Surely you jest. I don't think so, sweetheart. We'll be doing this my way."

Well, that's reassuring. Ziara had a feeling she was about to get a lesson in all things Sloan—and it would turn everything she'd planned for on its ear. She pulled out her handy-dandy tablet to take notes, since that seemed to be her only function here.

"We'll need new ideas, new designs, definitely a new designer," he said, his voice so matter-of-fact that she blinked for a moment, unable to handle the transition from sexy hunk to demanding boss that quickly. But she managed to pull herself together.

Then his words truly registered. Yikes! A new designer definitely would not go over well.

Sloan continued. "Something splashy. Something to draw in big buyers, get people talking, get them curious…"

He dropped into the chair behind his desk. "Presenting the line, one buyer at a time in the studio, is standard fare. We need a fireworks show, not a firecracker…I've got it!" Sloan jerked to his feet, palms slapping on his desk with enough force to startle her. "We'll bring fashion week right here to Atlanta, Georgia. We'll put on a fashion show." He started to pace, throwing ideas out with such enthusiasm that she found herself pulled into the spirit without even realizing it. Before she knew it, he had location ideas, preshow party ideas, guest list suggestions, and on and on until he ran out of steam about an hour later.

Ziara's fingers ached from typing so fast; even she had to concede to Sloan's intelligence. Once he latched onto an idea, he thought through every angle—catch, plus and minus. Very impressive. If he truly had plans to destroy Eternity Designs, he was going about it the wrong way.

Glancing up in the sudden silence, she found Sloan staring directly at her. She should have been alarmed, afraid of what he might see, but she had sunk so deeply under the spell of his voice that she merely floated.

His eyes widened at whatever he saw in her own, then

flashed with a heat that echoed deep inside her core. The connection remained taut for long moments as the heat gained momentum like a house afire.

Only when it threatened to burst out of control did Ziara panic. She bent her head to focus on the tablet still sitting in her lap. Though she felt hot enough for her fingers to burn it, the tablet was miraculously unsinged.

A new kind of heat enveloped her—embarrassment. As Sloan approached, her teeth worried her lower lip. Would he say something? Think she'd changed her mind about him? Think that she was silently asking him to come on to her? With her limited experience, she wasn't even sure what kind of message she'd just sent. As her imagination picked up speed, Sloan paused a few steps away.

Then he continued around his desk and sat with a squeak of leather. Out of the corner of her eye, she saw his elbows settle onto the arms of the chair as if familiar with the pose, his fingers forming a peak with his fingertips. Relief swept through her, a cooling breeze, though it couldn't extinguish the fire altogether. She chose to ignore it.

"So we'll be putting on a fall fashion show this year. You'll need to book the venue and start construction on the backdrop. Some plans can't be finalized until closer to the actual date, but pick out invitations, contact the modeling agency so we can line up models, all that stuff."

He leaned forward, his gaze seeing into the distance. "My focus will be on finding the right designer to carry out my ideas."

That was a discussion she'd prefer to postpone for, oh, forever. A new designer would shake the foundations of Eternity, regardless of how wonderful he was.

"And what would those ideas be?" she asked, poised to type. How was she going to tell Vivian all of this? Ziara was excited by some of the plans, but change was definitely not Vivian's forte.

Sloan grinned, resorting to his ample sex appeal in the blink of an eye. "Uh-uh. I'm not giving it up that easily."

Their eyes met and held. In the aftermath of their earlier connection, his bright blue gaze unnerved her more than ever. Not only did it threaten her internal control, it made her want to clamp the top of her jacket closed to hide every hint of cleavage. She pressed her thighs together in a purely feminine gesture of defense.

Slowly he rose and circled the desk, leaning his hips against the front. The angle allowed him to tower over her, while inadvertently giving her a level view of—

No, she wouldn't look. Her fight-or-flight instincts kicked in with a rush. She needed a few moments away from this man's disturbing sensuality. Heck, a few hours would be better. Rising to her feet, she said, "If that's all, I'll start—"

"Ziara."

Her fingers fiddled with her tablet while her gaze examined the polished floorboards.

"I expect hard work out of all my employees. I don't think that will be a problem with you. But trust…trust has to be earned, doesn't it?"

The guilt burned deep inside, because she knew she'd have to tell what she'd learned to Vivian—sooner rather than later. But it was her strong work ethic that just might tear her in two. Her dedication demanded she do what was right for Eternity Designs; her loyalty demanded she do anything Vivian asked of her.

"Though hiring and firing is Vivian's department for now," he continued, his voice deceptively benign, "be aware you wouldn't be in this office if I didn't want you to be." He stopped an arm's length from her, bringing the icy heat of his gaze closer, stinging her conscience. "You have your own reasons for being loyal to Vivian."

She heard the implied question behind his statement. She swallowed, the urge to speak unnerving. How could she describe all Vivian had done for her, the hands-on coaching and molding of her abilities? She opted for short and sweet.

"Vivian saw my willingness to do a job right, even as a simple secretary. To uphold the ideals of this company."

"Where tradition and style forever align," Sloan murmured.

A slight smile tugged her lips. Her chin lifted. She knew her intentions here were right, no matter what anyone else thought. Pride in her hard work, in pulling herself up from the bottom rung of the ladder, refused to let him condemn her loyalties. "Yes."

Sloan stepped even closer. The urge to retreat exploded in her belly. Her muscles jumped to high alert, tightening in preparation for flight.

"I, too, value hard work, initiative and loyalty." He paused, as if choosing his words carefully. "Just don't forget who you work for now."

The pressure of his stare proved too much with Vivian's expectations still flashing neon in Ziara's brain. Her gaze fell, grazing his fit body to the tips of his Gucci dress shoes. A short nod was all she could manage.

She wasn't likely to forget anything about Sloan.

Still, the need to push back rose. "Wanting to uphold the values of this company isn't a bad thing. After all, it is the way your father wanted this business run." She ignored the twinge of her conscience. The truth hurt. This time, she leaned closer to him. "People other than you are allowed to care about this place, you know."

Something flashed across his face that she couldn't quite read, but it encouraged her to push harder. Not for Vivian. Not for her job. For Eternity Designs. "If you would just tell me what you're trying to do here instead of leaving me in the dark, then maybe I could help."

He met her halfway, crowding into her personal space with a sexy grin. "You'll have to try harder than that to access my... secrets."

Three

Sloan took a deep breath and wrestled with his libido for a moment before managing to lock it down. How could the simple sounds of Ziara at her desk turn him into a dirty old man? Well, not quite old, if the level of urgency he felt was anything to go by.

They had a long day ahead—he was pretty sure she was going to hate him by the time he was done, but as the saying went, he had to get rid of the old to make room for the new.

He would need Ziara's help to carry out his plans without permanent damage. Robert and Anthony were indeed good designers, but designers who needed a serious shake-up. Vivian had offered Ziara for her expertise and he planned to conquer a large portion of his new territory today.

After a moment of silence, Ziara peeked around the door. "Do you need me for anything this morning, Mr. Creighton?"

Oh, honey, I need you for something really bad. Even though it was totally inappropriate, he couldn't tame the thought. Once again Ziara was wrapped in a narrow skirt and suit jacket, although this one was a dark chocolate-brown that complemented her eyes, bringing out the golden flecks with a glimpse of a silky gold camisole. A little better, though seeing her abundant hair pinned to the nape of her neck just made his hands itch to let it all loose.

He shifted in his seat. "I've got a full agenda today. Where do we stand so far?"

Ziara's efficiency impressed him. Not only had she started contacting people and places yesterday, she'd made a detailed list of the facts so he could compare easily and make decisions.

Old business out of the way, he straightened his shoulders, preparing to face the hardest part of the day. "Let's take a trip down to the design floor and see what's what with the Old Brigade."

The *Old Brigade* was the employees' term for the two main designers who headed and vetted all the dress designs for the company. Though by no means original, they'd each been with the company for over fifteen years.

Ziara hesitated, frozen for a moment like a deer caught in headlights at dusk; then she gathered her tablet and smoothed down her skirt.

He let her maintain her silence as they crossed into the hall, but he couldn't afford for her to hold back. Everything might as well be out in the open.

He stopped in the middle of the deserted hallway. "Look, Ziara," he said, turning to face her. "One of the reasons you're here is to help me with intercompany relations, schedules, procedures, et cetera. Right?"

"Yes, Mr. Creighton."

The prim purse of her full mouth had his brows rising, a grin tugging at his lips. "Didn't we decide on Sloan? After all, over the next three months, we're going to be spending a helluva lot of time together."

Her lips tightened a touch more before she conceded. "Yes, Sloan."

Teasing her out of that "strictly business" attitude was way too much fun. "Now, I can't do my job if you don't do your job—"

A weighty protest formed in her eyes, though her face remained calm. This woman's responses were seriously under wraps. He had to look very closely to catch the signals, but they told him some genuinely hot emotions hid beneath the surface. "Don't get me wrong, you've been very helpful. But I need an honest rundown of what I'm facing on the design floor today."

"I—I—"

"Honesty. Right now. Got it?"

"Why do you need my opinion? You said you'd been here often as a child."

"And as a child I noticed the person most important to me— my father, and the place I spent the most time—his office. The rest? Not so much. I haven't set foot on the design floor since I was ten."

Her gaze zeroed in on his face for a moment, then she spoke. "Anthony and Robert are very talented designers."

Keeping his irritation from showing proved a little easier beneath her disapproving glare.

"The trouble will come from Robert—he's ruled the design floor through talent and overpowering personality for years. Anthony's a sweetheart, but don't take his lack of attitude for subservience. He's soaking it all in, processing it in his own time and making his own decisions."

He grinned. "That wasn't so bad, was it?"

The low growl from her throat surprised him, sending a shock of sensation right where he didn't need it. *Keep it light. Best to just move on.* "Let's go." But he was getting a really good idea how to provoke her into an honest response.

Just irritate her beyond measure.

The elevator took them down to the third floor and they stepped out onto the observation deck. The design department occupied most of the second floor, but the large exhibition space below could be viewed and accessed from the open walkway they now occupied.

As he and Ziara made their way down the spiral staircase, Ziara's heels clicking on the metal steps, the designers appeared to be gearing up for the day.

"Ziara," Robert exclaimed as she descended the last two steps. "What brings you to our little kingdom?"

Anthony simply smiled and wrapped her in a half hug. Her smile was natural and easy, but she didn't return the touch. *Interesting.*

"I wanted to introduce y'all to Mrs. Creighton's stepson, Sloan Creighton."

The designers exchanged a look, but it didn't display as much alarm as Sloan had anticipated. Nor resignation, either. His Spidey senses started to tingle.

"Yes, yes," Robert said, leading the way by offering his hand. "I believe I remember James mentioning you to us, *Dieu ait son âme.*"

God rest his soul, indeed. Out of the corner of his eye, Sloan could see Ziara glance his way. Since it was obvious from their benign reception that neither designer had a clue what was coming down the pike, Sloan decided to play along.

"Vivian tells me you two are working on the fall line. I'd love to see the best of Eternity's upcoming designs," he said, ignoring Ziara's sudden stare.

The men were only too happy to show off. Too bad they didn't realize they were arming him to take them both down. They exchanged excited glances, then walked toward the display boards in unison.

Sloan stepped closer to Ziara as they followed. "Just relax and follow my lead," he murmured from the corner of his mouth.

After listening to Robert expound on the sketches for over half an hour, Sloan was definitely unimpressed. Just as he imagined their buyer had been.

When Robert finally wound down, Sloan's voice filled the stillness. "Did you listen to anything that buyer said?"

The men stiffened, but there wasn't anything they could say in their own defense.

Sloan pushed forward. "She said the designs were stale. She said the dresses were old-fashioned. Not classic. Not retro. Those are buzz words. Compliments. Stale is not." He gestured toward the stack of drawings. "Nothing has changed here. Nothing. I can find this same thing in any bridal magazine—from ten years ago."

"How would you know what the buyer said?" Anthony asked, his voice sounding weak after the booming quality of Robert's.

"And who do you think you are, to come in here and criticize our work?" Robert added.

"I am now the creative director of Eternity Designs's fall line. From here on out, all decisions from this department must be approved solely by me."

The silence was so absolute it rang loud in his ears. Robert's face gradually turned a shade of purple and Anthony's eyes flicked back and forth between the other people in the room as if he expected someone to tell him what was really going on here.

Finally Robert spoke, his voice coming from deep in his barreled chest. "Ziara, if this is a joke, it isn't funny."

"He isn't kidding, Robert," she said in her most soothing voice.

"Look," Sloan said, impatient with the theatrics. "We have a lot to do and a very short time to do it in. Whether you were informed of this decision previously is not my problem. Getting Eternity Designs back on track is—and I'll be doing it my way."

"Why would we need—"

"Are you truly going to pretend you don't know why I'm here?" Sloan met Robert's blustery gaze directly. "You may not pay much attention to financial statements while you're down here in fantasyland, but I know for a fact you were present when the Bridal Boutique buyer ripped your designs apart. Would you like me to go into more detail, or do you remember it for yourself?"

Anthony again joined the conversation. "No, we remember it well enough."

"Good. I am here to get Eternity back in the black and at

the forefront of the wedding apparel industry. So for the next three months you will answer to me—and only me."

"We won't do it," Robert insisted. "After thirty years as a designer, I refuse to have my ideas approved by an amateur."

"Then I'll bring in someone who will."

Harsh. But he knew from his own history that sometimes the hardest lessons were the most memorable…if you used them to your advantage. Just like he'd turned his father's rejection into professional success.

Moving swiftly across the space, Sloan lifted the entire stack of drawings and dumped them into a nearby trash can. "Start over."

Ziara and Anthony gasped at the same time. But it was Robert he continued to focus on, the leader of this little group. Bring him to heel and the rest would follow.

Robert sputtered his indignation while Anthony's face crumpled as if he was going to cry. How in the world could he get through to these yahoos?

Sloan didn't anticipate Ziara's sudden tight grip on his arm. She pulled him out of hearing range and turned to face him.

"Do you really think this is the way to gain their cooperation?"

He tried to focus on her words, but his own frustration quickly morphed into desire as she moved close enough for them to hear each other without eavesdroppers. All that solid, testosterone-induced drive melted into liquid desire that pounded in his veins with a thrumming rhythm. Lord have mercy, how had this woman gotten under his skin so quickly?

"I don't need their cooperation. If they don't do what I tell them, they're out of here."

A repressive frown marred those full lips. "Robert and Anthony have always been the stars of Eternity Designs. You should treat them with more respect."

How could those lips, pressed tight like a disapproving schoolmarm's, still come across as sexy? He was actually struggling to follow her words. Him. The king of keeping things professional.

"Don't you see, Ziara, that's the problem," he finally managed. "They've had people kissing their asses for years, with no challenges to their work. They think they can give a minimal effort and still be put on a pedestal. And Eternity suffers for it."

"They do work—"

He could almost kiss her for the concern in the dark depths of her eyes but it was misplaced. "Not enough. Where's the market research, the fresh, new ideas? They don't just happen by playing around all day. Continued success takes more effort."

Understanding made a reluctant appearance in her gorgeous brown eyes. For some reason it made all the difference in the world to him. "I know I sound harsh. But they're grown men who've been catered to for years. A polite request isn't going to even make a dent." Reaching out, he brushed his thumb along the softened curve of her jaw. "I do have a method behind my madness, I promise."

The feel of her silky skin beneath his touch was magic, along with the warmth and subtle catch of her breath. They both froze in surprise for a moment. It was all Sloan could do to resist brushing his lips over the same spot.

Whoa. This was the design floor, not a nightclub…not even the privacy of his office. And judging by the utter silence laced with antagonism behind his back, Sloan knew *Robert* wouldn't hesitate to throw around accusations of sexual misconduct. With Ziara's approval or without it.

He took a careful step back, letting his hand drop to his side. "Just remember something—I wouldn't be here if they'd been doing their jobs right in the first place. Okay?"

Her nod was firm, though her eyes were still a little dazed.

This meeting needed to get back on track. "Ziara," he snapped, but with a little less bite than he'd used on the men. "The tablet, please."

She hurried to obey, giving him a moment to regain his focus before turning back to the others. When she handed over the device, he noticed the care she took not to touch him again.

After a moment of tapping on the smooth surface, he paused, looking up at the group around him.

"Current trends favor retro designs, new twists on the old, avant-garde as well as classic." During his recent research, he'd seen some unique retro looks in the fashion and wedding magazines, and they had sparked his own creative imagination.

"In less than three months, I'll be showcasing our newest designs during a professional fashion show. We're going to bring fashion week right here to Atlanta. It'll be an exclusive, invitation-only event that I want people talking about for months."

As Sloan continued to explain the fall show, excitement crept over the anger that had tightened the designers' faces. He might have punctured their egos earlier, but now he was tempting them.

Lifting the tablet, he turned it around to face them. "Every event needs a theme, a focal point. This is ours."

"A car? Are you insane?" Robert yelled, returning to his angry disbelief.

"Not just any car, a Rolls-Royce. A classic car epitomizing the elegance, sleek design and subtle sensuality of the late 1930s. An era where women flaunted sexy curves, draped their bodies with fabrics that showcased their femininity, and set out to entice the opposite sex. Think of the actresses of the time— Marlene Dietrich, Mae West, Vivian Leigh. The dresses they wore—the draped material, exposed backs…"

He caught a glimmer of understanding in Ziara's eyes. Knowledge of where he was going with this idea.

"Ridiculous," Robert insisted. "This is the stupidest thing I've heard in my lifetime."

Sloan wasn't backing down. "We're going to do this and do it right. Get on board, or jump overboard. Your choice."

When had work started feeling like a taffy puller?

Ziara waited until Sloan left the building for lunch before heading to Vivian's office. Her stomach cramped, knowing Vivian would have already heard about the upcoming show, but also knowing she couldn't blatantly walk out of Sloan's office straight to his stepmother's.

Observing Sloan for two days had taught her one thing already—he wasn't playing. His knowledge this morning showed he had done his homework on the market, design, themes, even fashion shows. He'd been calm but firm, occasionally harsh, with Robert and Anthony. Stepping solidly into a leadership role, even if he had to do it by force.

Most disturbing of all, his ideas for the show intrigued her.

With some organization, this could be an incredibly successful event, one the upper classes of Atlanta society would flock to in droves. Eternity Designs would be on the tip of everyone's tongues and the front page in the society section. Notable brides would once again be drawn to the showroom for one-of-a-kind dresses.

But to her shame, Sloan's appeal continued to taunt her on a more physical level. Vivian had insisted she was the last woman who would be tempted by Sloan's charm, but the need that had crawled into her body at his singular touch frightened her. She'd seen her mother move from man to man, taking whatever they could give her, using her body to manipulate them. Mixing business with pleasure was the last thing Ziara wanted in her life. The level of temptation here actually scared her bone deep.

Abigail gave her a sympathetic look as she entered the room. "She's waiting on you, Ziara."

I bet she is. Her hand pausing on the doorknob, Ziara only let herself hesitate a second before going in.

"Ah, Ziara," Vivian said from behind her antique desk. "I see you have finally deigned to bring me news."

Vivian gestured for her to sit. The walk across the room distracted Ziara from the uneasiness caused by Vivian's words. "I felt it appropriate to wait until Sloan left for lunch—"

"Why? He's surely aware that one of your jobs is to keep me informed. Next time I want to hear it from you, rather than the office grapevine."

Yes, but I couldn't bring myself to rub my choices in his face.

She'd probably heard from the Old Brigade, who'd run to Vivian to tattle the minute they'd realized they were losing control.

Ziara wondered if they remembered Vivian had once been a mere secretary—and how long it had taken them to accept the new order of things when she took over. Given the evidence from this morning, Ziara didn't think acceptance had come quickly.

"I'm very excited about this new idea for the line's presentation," she started.

"Ah yes, the fashion show. I hate to admit it, but I'm seeing the merits of this plan myself. I want a full report."

"I've just started working on the details. I'm looking into venues, modeling agencies and such."

"Keep me informed as everything takes shape."

Ziara murmured, "Yes, ma'am," under her breath, but Vivian was already moving on.

"Make it good. Getting some choice buyers in here will make this the must-have ticket of the fall season. I'll have Abigail get you a list of contacts, and I want to know as soon as the RSVPs come in."

If Sloan was a train squishing her on the tracks, Vivian was a wrecking ball, destroying Ziara's calm handling of this difficult assignment. Her mentor ran through a laundry list of items she wanted Ziara to check into, almost doubling the amount of work Sloan had given her. She saw quite a few late nights in her near future.

"Since you will be in the thick of all of this, Ziara—" Vivian's spine straightened as if bracing herself for what was to come "—you should know...if our largest buyer pulls her orders, as she has threatened if the line doesn't move in a more modern, unique direction, it will put the company in a very disadvantageous financial position."

Even Vivian's attempt at genteel diplomacy couldn't hide the facts: Eternity Designs was in deep financial trouble. The confirmation of the actual problem had Ziara's stomach dropping like it would on a roller coaster, a ride she avoided getting on at all costs.

Coming to work here, helping to build some of the finest dresses and dreams, had been like finding her true home. She wasn't ready to leave.

Vivian's fingers spun her wedding band in an endless circle. "So you can see how very important it is for the fall line to be not just good, but spectacular. By putting you in his office, I can let Sloan think he's in charge until we see what he decides to do with the fall line." Vivian's heeled pump set up a twitchy rhythm. "I've known him for a long time. He's sneaky, deceptive. His mother's lower-class roots are showing, I guess."

Ziara controlled the surprise that threatened to bloom on her face. Social standing had always been important to Vivian, but Ziara had never before seen evidence of prejudice.

"I know you said he was rebellious as a teenager." Perfectly normal, in Ziara's opinion. "Why would you think he's up to something now?"

Being on the receiving end of Vivian's glare wasn't comfortable.

"Haven't you ever heard that a leopard never changes its spots?" Vivian asked. "Besides, there are rumors that he uses some rather ruthless tactics to get his way these days." Her pen tapped against her desk. One thump, then two. "He's up to something," she continued. "And I need to stay on top of it. *You* need to stay on top of it."

Ziara wasn't sure if the turmoil gaining ground in her gut was troubled conscience or the guilt of temptation, but she couldn't simply ignore it. "Vivian, I really, well, I simply think that someone else might be more suited to working with Sl—Mr. Creighton. I could easily coordinate the show details from—"

"His office. That's where I put you and that's where you will stay. Or is there some reason you would request a change?"

The last thing Ziara wanted to do was explain the ins and outs of the past two days. If only she could make Vivian understand… "Honestly, I don't feel very comfortable with the position I'm in. If you think Sloan will stop anything he's doing because of me, well, he won't. I just—"

Vivian's head tilted slightly to the side, her brown eyes studying Ziara with sudden intensity. For the first time in a long time, Ziara wanted to hide from her boss, to squirrel away the reactions she had to Sloan just as she had the secrets of her past. Vivian would never accept her if she knew either one.

"Have I not done enough for you, Ziara?"

Not expecting the attack, Ziara found herself speechless.

"Have I not taught you all that I can about running this business, about behaving professionally, about coming out ahead of those not willing to put every ounce of effort into their jobs?"

"Yes, ma'am. You've been more than generous."

"Then why do I suddenly feel like all of that effort has been wasted on the wrong person?"

Panic shot deep, mixing with the fear Ziara carried on a daily basis: that one day, everything she'd worked so hard for would crash down into a pile of rubble. She would not go back to being the uneducated girl condemned by everyone around her.

"I certainly don't want you to feel that way," Ziara said over the pounding of her heart. "I'm very grateful—"

"I see plenty, Ziara," Vivian snapped, her eyes as harsh as her tone. "And what I'm seeing isn't gratitude, understand?"

Knowing she'd overstepped Vivian's invisible limit, Ziara conceded quickly. "Yes, ma'am."

"You've worked very hard to get where you are, Ziara. That's why I chose you to succeed Abigail as my executive assistant when she retires later this year."

At the praise, a glow bloomed beneath her fear. She'd yearned to be recognized for her accomplishments for as long as she could remember. First at school, then at community college, from her first job till now. Though she hadn't found validation at home, her move to Atlanta had been the start of a whole new life.

"I'm confident that you'll do what's best for Eternity Designs." Vivian stood, her posture and classically tailored business suit a picture of authority. Ziara moved quickly to join her.

"This position, though difficult, will also be excellent training for you, and I don't have to worry about the Creighton good looks turning your head like some of the less dedicated girls around here. Do I?"

Ziara realized the question was rhetorical, so she simply shook her head, keeping her growing doubts to herself. Oh, she had no intention of falling into bed with a man like Sloan Creighton. On the other hand, how did she keep his charm and obvious business smarts from influencing her away from what Vivian wanted?

Vivian moved on, unaware of Ziara's fears. "By the time we come out of this, Eternity Designs will be set for the future. I'll be in charge, and you'll have that job as my E.A."

Ziara shifted in her heels. "But what if he succeeds? How can you risk him gaining a majority's ownership if you don't trust him?"

Vivian turned away, her face hidden as she crossed to the window. "Don't worry," she said, twisting her wedding ring around her finger again. "I'll take care of that."

Knowing she'd been dismissed, Ziara retreated to the safety of the outer office, where Abigail waited with a kind smile and some lists.

"Thank you, Abigail."

"No problem, sweetie. Just let me know if you have any questions."

How about, *Will I make it through this without losing my freakin' mind?* Or, *Is everyone going to hate me before this show is over?* But she said nothing, conscious for once of exactly how alone she was.

Walking through the doorway, she found Sloan leaning against her desk. Her stomach dropped to her toes and a flush suffused her cheeks. The guilt was probably glaring out from her downcast gaze and shifting feet.

Where was this guilt coming from? A shot of surprise jolted through her at the answer. The guilt didn't stem from tattling like a four-year-old. That was the best thing for Eternity Designs…for now. She simply didn't want to face him knowing she'd tried to get out of working with him. Her feet stuttered to stillness and she swallowed, praying her voice would work at this point. "May I help you with something, Mr. Creighton?"

Those bright blue eyes, so full of life earlier today, were now cold enough to freeze the devil himself in his tracks. His mouth crooked up on one side, his boyish good looks now brittle around the edges. Oh yeah, he knew what she was up to, and there was no defense against that knowledge.

"I don't know why I'm surprised."

For some unknown reason, she couldn't brush this moment aside with professionalism or tactful confusion. "I don't know, either. You told me you understood my duties here."

"That doesn't mean I have to like it."

Me, either.

Ziara struggled to return to that place where she was strictly a secretary performing an assigned task, but she couldn't. Some kind of barrier had been breached with his touch earlier today, and she was very afraid there was no going back from it.

She had the distinct feeling he wouldn't let her go back even if she tried. His next words confirmed her suspicions. "Too bad I can't give you what you really deserve."

"And what would that be?" she asked, though the naughty mischief melting the iceberg should have warned her she'd moved into dangerous territory.

"A spanking."

Four

The next few days went by relatively smoothly as Ziara discovered the ins and outs of working for Sloan Creighton.

He liked his coffee black with just a touch of sugar for sweetness, but he only drank it in the morning. After eleven, he switched to Mountain Dew. He came into the office around nine-thirty every morning, smelling of citrus and a spicy undertone after his daily game of racquetball. He paced while he dictated letters, his long legs performing for her benefit alone. While dreaming up new show ideas, he liked to lean back in his chair with his Gucci-clad feet propped on the edge of the desk.

She often caught a glimpse of him standing at those floor-to-ceiling windows watching people walk by five stories below, deep enough in thought that she'd close the door behind her with extra force to remind him of her presence.

She was getting to know him way too well.

This new knowledge was uncomfortable, but not as uncomfortable as the suspicion that he was cataloging some things about her, as well. Those damn eyes! Not to mention the occasional spicy remark, like that spanking comment, that she pretended to ignore no matter how outrageous he got. The last thing he needed was encouragement.

Today shattered the routine when Sloan hit the outer door like a bull. She hadn't seen that controlled anger since his first day, that contained heat he'd wielded against Vivian like a fine-tuned weapon.

"I've got a lot of calls to make, Ziara. Don't bother me."

"Yes, Mr. Creighton," she said reverting to formality in her confusion. She watched those long strides carry him into his office, the door slamming behind him. Definitely a good day to keep her head down and work on clearing the clutter from her desk.

A few hours of muffled yelling and banging later, she decided now was probably a good time to escape. She made her way through the corridors to the design floor. Anthony met her a few feet in with a quick and quiet hug. He knew exactly why she was here. Leading her across the room, he showed her the new shipment of sample materials scattered across a large table.

"Robert is very upset with me," he said. "He thinks I'm a sellout."

Ziara glanced over his shoulder at the normally boisterous man now sitting quietly at a drafting table. "Why would he think that?" she asked, keeping her voice low to match Anthony's.

He gestured toward the materials. "Because I ordered these."

Ziara took in the mixtures of cream, pinks, barely there blues and an almost yellow color on a display table that was normally white, white and white. "Hmm. I can see where that would be a problem."

"I've tried to move Robert in new directions for years now, especially as grumblings surfaced from the buyers. But he just won't listen."

"I don't think Mr. Creighton will give him that option."

"Well, maybe he will succeed where I have failed." With a sad smile, he wandered back across the room, leaving Ziara alone for what he knew was her favorite pastime.

Picking up the nearby invoices, she started matching the

materials on the table with the names and prices on the sheets of paper. She studied the fresh array of colors, the textures, drape and a myriad of other things.

In an ideal world—where she would have had a supportive family, scholarships and no need to be her own sole support immediately after getting her GED—she would have been a supplier, searching out the finest materials, the best deals for the entire company in accessories, gemstones, beading, lining, everything. As it was, she could spend hours immersed in the research but allowed herself only small windows here and there. Luckily Anthony wasn't threatened by her presence or interest, so he'd spent many a minute teaching her bits and pieces. Bless his heart.

"Enjoying yourself?"

Ziara froze, her hand buried in a pile of pink-tinged satin. To her knowledge, Vivian didn't know about her little visits here. Yet it hadn't taken Sloan a week to uncover her secret.

"I'm sorry, Mr. Creigh—um, Sloan. Did you need me for something?"

When he squeezed the back of his neck as if to relieve the tension gathered there, she couldn't help but sympathize.

"I definitely need you, Ziara. Don't you know that?"

Her gaze zeroed in on his face, searching for the intention behind the words. His bright blue eyes were now tired, but a shiver of awareness still snuck down her spine. No matter how he looked, no matter what he said, she felt he was bringing her to an awareness of him as a man—and herself as a woman.

She murmured, "I'm happy to oblige." Then cringed inside at the many ways her words could be misinterpreted. She straightened as he moved closer. He reached toward her stomach, which tightened in anticipation—but his hand bypassed her to explore the materials on the table beyond.

A smoky-blue chiffon, almost gray, held his attention. "Very nice," he murmured, the sound almost seductive, as though he was encouraging…something. He lifted the material, testing the feel, weight and drape.

His hands fascinated her, the long fingers with their neatly clipped nails a sharp contrast to the fragile-looking material. But his eyes drew her, too. Those bright blues had darkened as if he were looking inward rather than at the material he handled so skillfully.

"What is this?" he asked.

"It's a light chiffon, mostly used for accents and layering," she said.

Snapping out of his thoughts, he glanced at her in surprise. "Been studying your materials, have you?"

Warmth flooded into her cheeks and chest. "Anthony has been teaching me."

Rather than the condemnation she'd expected, his eyes softened in appreciation. "Show me."

Sloan found himself entranced as Ziara explained the contrasts between silks, chiffons, satins and numerous other materials used in dressmaking. Not over the information itself, even though it was appreciated, but the unguarded spark in her eyes.

Then there was the show: her slender arms lifting each material to demonstrate its ability to drape, the thickness and what it might be used for.

"You could have been a supplier," he said, drawn in by her enthusiasm.

The stillness that invaded her body told him he'd hit a sore spot, even though her lowered lashes hid her expression from him. Not quite understanding, he asked, "Why didn't you? This stuff obviously interests you."

The muscles around her mouth tightened, then she raised her guarded gaze. "Fashion production and supply chain management degrees don't come cheap." She started sorting the material by color. "Tuition was nonexistent for me, so that type of dream wasn't even on the table. I looked at my options and chose what worked with my skills. It wasn't until I came here that I realized how interesting this side of the business could be."

"Your parents weren't able to help?"

Her mouth twisted. "Not even close. It was just my mother and me, anyway. She didn't think school was worth much."

"What about your guidance counselor? If your grades were good, scholarships could have helped."

"Maybe in another life."

The spark of curiosity that ran through his body was exciting but dangerous. He took the leap, anyway. "Why?"

Finally she stopped rearranging the material so she could glare at him. "Look. I came from a really small town, even more southern than Atlanta, with not enough money and very few options. I worked my way through secretarial school with two jobs, eating peanut butter from a spoon every night. Not everyone needs a high salary and trust fund to be successful."

That should have stung—and it did, but not in the personal way he expected. He could see how hard she must have worked to attain her level of success at such a young age—which meant this wasn't just a job to her.

She wasn't just Vivian's pet.

He couldn't think about what that meant to his plans. So he let his mind conjure pictures of her caressing the fabric. Within seconds, he began to visualize designs: a sleek gown of pale pink satin, almost bright against her dark skin, drifting low over her naked back, accented with white diamonds and silver thread. The smoky chiffon shaped into three-dimensional flowers at the shoulders of a structured gray, almost silver, silk dress. The creamy yellow draped tight across her torso in tiny pleats that met at the curve of her hip, then released into a waterfall of softly lilting, creamy white feathers.

All of them made exclusively for the incredible body before him.

His horrible morning dissolved under the rush of creative energy.

"What are you thinking?" he heard her say, her voice echoing slightly as she pulled him from his own head, that place where he created all the things he needed, wanted, with the easy strokes of his mind.

It didn't matter whether it was building plans, an office design, extensive renovations…or, apparently, wedding dresses. He had only to envision it and the lines appeared in the forefront of his mind. It was very helpful, incredibly productive and totally intoxicating.

Which was the only explanation he had for what he did next. Reaching around her to the desk, he snagged paper and a drawing pencil. The move brought him flush with her side, prompting a surge of heat wherever their bodies met, though he forced himself to move away quickly.

He could tell she felt it, too, by the widening of her eyes and the way she held her breath. He shoved the materials on the table aside and started to draw. Within minutes, he had a simple outline of the pink satin dress he'd imagined, though he kept the distinctive characteristics of the model vague.

"Wow," she breathed. "That's gorgeous."

"Thank you."

Her smile warmed him, intoxicating in its sincerity. He often had the feeling that she simply responded to him the way she should, the way an assistant was expected to respond to her boss. Not this time.

Fire lurked beneath the surface of this buttoned-down babe, and he desperately wanted to release it—even if he was her boss.

"I mean it," he continued, anxious to avoid the temptation of his thoughts. "You've shown me exactly what I need."

Before he could do something stupid like kiss those full red lips, he pivoted on his heel and walked away. Now that he had a direction, he knew just how to carry it out.

Eternity Designs would never be the same.

Sloan stalked down the hall toward the elevators, the adrenaline still thrumming through his veins. Pictures of Ziara racing through his mind.

"How's your new assistant working out, Sloan?"

Damn it. He'd been so close to the open doorway!

He pivoted to find Vivian standing in the shadows. Had she been waiting for him to walk by? Had she watched as he and Ziara talked?

"Great choice, Vivian. She'll serve me just fine, I think."

Vivian studied him with the same barely tolerant expression she'd used after many of his teenage escapades. "What's wrong?"

Ah, the pitfalls of working with someone who'd watched him grow up. He moved a few steps closer. Lowering his voice, he tightened his control over the high levels of excitement, frustration and arousal still surging through his veins.

"It won't work, Vivian. Whatever reason you have for planting Ziara in my office—it won't work. I'm still going to do what I think is best for Eternity."

Patronizing was the only way to describe her smile. "I know exactly where Ziara's loyalties lie. She'll do the job I gave her."

"I'm going ahead with my plans, regardless." The feel of the sketch held securely in his grasp brought a surge of certainty. He was on the right path; now he needed the one person who would help him carry it out.

"So you've talked the Old Brigade into actually carrying out your crazy theme?" she asked, concern dampening her smug demeanor. Ah, she'd be so happy if he was stuck working with her two lackeys, wouldn't she?

"Robert and Anthony will fall in line soon enough." His chest tightened as all his earlier frustration rushed forward again.

She shook her head slowly. "Not according to Robert—I believe his exact words were 'over my dead body.'"

Her smug expression shattered his control like nothing else could have. "I wouldn't get too tickled if I were you."

"And why is that?"

"I'm about to turn Eternity Designs upside down."

The *ding* of the elevator signaled his escape. Sloan strode through the doors and turned back to see Vivian's perplexed expression just as they closed.

Five

Ziara dished up her quick version of paella into an oversize, bright green bowl, pausing a moment to inhale the spicy scent of peppers, andouille sausage and shrimp. Padding across to the table, she savored the coolness of the tiled kitchen floor on her bare feet.

After a long, deep drink of sweetened tea, she picked up her book in one hand and her fork in the other. Having survived her rough day at work, her mind craved the relaxing and safe surroundings of home. An early start to her weekend.

She'd worked so hard for her house and turned it into her very own sanctuary. Most important, it was as far from the environment she'd grown up in as possible.

Only here could she let down the defenses. She could safely indulge her passion for cooking, love of reading and flair for color.

She desperately needed that in the aftermath of her confusing response to her boss. Sloan was flirty, no doubt about it, but she'd always held herself to a higher standard. To think a few smiles, some genuine listening and one hot touch could turn her sensible head made her very angry—with herself.

The first bite of paella ignited a burn on her tongue that spread like flash fire up the walls of her mouth to the roof and inner edge of her lips. Yummy, but she suspected her turbulent thoughts had made her heavy-handed with the spices.

Ziara jumped at the jangle of the doorbell. She rarely had visitors—no family, no close friends. It was only five, so it was still fairly light out. Daylight savings time wouldn't hit for another month. Maybe it was a salesman or one of the neighbors' kids fund-raising for school. She sighed.

Traversing the short hallway linking the kitchen with the living room, Ziara paused to glance through the small window that ran down the side of the door. She wasn't above pretending she wasn't home.

The silhouette on the other side didn't quite register at first except to look vaguely familiar. Then, in an instant, it felt as if the heat from the paella exploded at the base of her neck and spread along her skull. Surely that wasn't Sloan so casually posed in the shade of her front porch?

She jerked back, suddenly vulnerable in her cotton yoga pants and old T-shirt, so thin it offered little to no coverage.

Cringing when the doorbell rang again, she looked up to find Sloan blocking the view from the window. Well, he knew she was here. Good manners insisted she open the door and see what he wanted. Muttering under her breath, she decided she now had a very personal reason for being irritated.

Grasping the cool metal of the knob, she pulled the door open just enough to see his handsome face.

"Sloan," she said, her voice more a question than an acknowledgment. She didn't issue an invitation, but apparently he didn't need one. Placing his palm flat on the door, he pushed inside, walking by her as if coming in was his right. She stood dumbfounded for a moment, then closed the door and leaned back against it, her arms crossed beneath breasts that tingled in his presence—without her permission.

"To what do I owe the pleasure?"

Her tone implied that seeing him was as far from a pleasure as she could get. She'd been well on the road to relaxation, but now her back was military straight and the muscles on each side of her neck tightened in protest. Even worse, she couldn't decide if it was because she didn't want him here... or because she did.

"Hi." He flashed his usual confident smile.

Up went her brow. He studied her expression with interest before his gaze moved to his surroundings.

A sense of invasion rose from the pit of her stomach, overriding the awareness that always seemed to come with his presence. She shifted uneasily as he walked around the room, gliding a finger along her favorite fleece throw and pausing to examine the exotic lines of the dancer in the picture over the mantel.

"Sloan," she said when the tension ratcheted up to an unbearable high, "what are you doing here?"

He faced her, his calm expression mocking the tremble that had slipped into her voice.

"I'll tell you," he said, "if you give me a plate of whatever smells so good. Suddenly I'm very hungry."

No, her mind screamed. She didn't want his presence lingering in her home, but short of pushing him back out the door, she had no idea how to refuse.

Sucking in a deep breath, she led the way back to the kitchen, ultraconscious as she passed him of the air grazing her bare arms and the gentle slap of her feet on the uncarpeted floors.

Crossing to the cabinet, she decided she might as well comply and find out what was going on. With efficient movements, she fixed him a plate and drink before settling him at the opposite end of the table from her. She ignored the smirk on his face as she returned to her seat.

He lifted his fork, then sniffed appreciatively before meeting her eyes.

"I know the perfect designer."

"I wasn't aware we needed one. We already have two." His

knowing look had her admitting, "Okay, we have at least one willing to help."

"But I've figured out the one person who can bring my vision to life."

His epiphany obviously accounted for the change in his mood, but not his presence—his most unwanted presence—here. "I'm glad. Couldn't this have waited until Monday?"

He shook his head, then hefted a heaping forkful of rice and spicy meat to his mouth. It had to be a sin to watch those sculpted lips close around anything, even something as innocent as a fork.

She didn't warn him about the heat. He'd probably just blow it off with some macho line. Besides, he was part of what had led to all that spice in the first place.

Suddenly his eyes widened and he coughed, just managing to keep the food in his mouth long enough to swallow. She leaned back with a feeling of satisfaction as his hand shot out for his glass. That would teach him not to push his way in where he wasn't wanted.

"Wow," he said after a long drink of iced tea, "that packs a wallop."

Watching him dig back in without a hint of hesitation, she thought, *Yes, it does.* "I'm glad you like it," she murmured, instead.

He cleared most of his plate, all the while studying her with intent looks that burned more than the food burned her mouth. Goose bumps spread along her skin despite the heat of the food.

She pushed her long hair back behind her shoulders, licking her dry, spicy lips. "Does Vivian approve of the new designer?"

"On the contrary, she'd have a very genteel hissy fit if she knew who he was."

She hesitated. Her gaze locked on her nearly empty plate before braving another glance at him. "So you haven't discussed this with her?"

He shook his head, waves of dark blond hair caressing the masculine angles of his face. "I don't plan to clue her in anytime soon." He leaned forward. "Do you?"

She leaned forward, too. "Let's get one thing straight. Whatever actions I take are for the good of the company. Convince me of the merits of your plan, and you won't have to worry about where my loyalties lie."

He stood, prowling around the sunny kitchen. His cool good looks blended with the greens and golds, the blue accents a reflection of his eyes, the pine cabinets just a touch lighter than his hair. He looked as if he belonged in this room.

He was testing her, but instead of resentment, an excited rush sizzled inside.

"This place isn't anything like I'd imagined," he said out of the blue.

As he took in the kitchen and her in one sweep, she wished for the ability to snap her fingers and be wearing a business suit instead of her relax-and-cook gear.

In an attempt to repress more personal discussions, she said, "I can't think why you'd wonder about it at all."

He stalked across the room and reached out to touch a strand of her loose hair that had fallen forward over her shoulder. "Who knew you had so much to hide."

Her quick intake of breath was her only outward response, but inside she mentally retreated. She couldn't afford to let him in on her secrets if she wanted to remain a respectable part of his business. Knowing would change everything. It always did. The few she'd told her deepest feelings to had turned their backs on her in an instant, and then she'd learned the golden rule of silence.

Standing, she stalked back down the hall and pulled the door open, not so discreetly inviting him to leave.

He followed, the soft-soled boots he wore silent on the wood floor, his face unreadable. Pulling a card from his wallet, he scribbled on the back. "Here's my cell phone number in case you need to contact me."

She stared blankly at the card in his hand. "Aren't you coming into the office on Monday?"

"No," he said. "And neither are you."

"Why not?"

That sexy grin was back. "Pack your bags. We're going to Vegas."

Six

Sloan arrived at the airport with plenty of time to spare. He eased through security, then settled in to wait. Ziara seemed the type to arrive early, but after last night he realized he didn't know a thing about her. Not the real Ziara. Underneath that cool, businesslike exterior lurked a woman he suspected burned as hot as her paella. That intrigued him. What intrigued him more was the *why*.

Why was she so different at work? This wasn't a case of the same woman just acting on a more professional level. No, this was two totally different women.

The rich, resonant colors in the living room—burgundy, flaming oranges and yellows, deep purple accented with gold—seemed such a natural setting for her dark beauty. Why would she dress down in drab grays, browns and navies?

That hair, soft around her face, a silky waterfall draping her chest and shoulders, made him want to spread it across a pillow or, better yet, across his chest. Of course, if she was hoping to disguise her thick, satin glory, she'd failed. Pulling it up to the crown of her head as she did at work only emphasized the exotic slant of her eyes and the exquisite lines of her cheekbones.

Did she get her spicy, riveting beauty from her mother? In all the simple elegance of her home, Sloan hadn't seen one personal photograph on display—not one of Ziara or any family, which struck him as odd.

He glanced over to see her standing in line for security. Looking at his watch, he realized she'd waited until the last moment to arrive. He smiled. Now that he knew what was inside, he wouldn't let her revert back to "all business."

A familiar ache built throughout his body as he watched her progress across the waiting area. The whoosh of adrenaline was similar to the rush of creativity, only a thousand times stronger. He no longer just wanted this woman—he *had* to have her. Which was a problem, because he was technically her boss. Temporarily. Although, if she was also his lover, then he'd know exactly where her loyalties lay. He could live with that…couldn't he?

"Good morning, Sloan," she said, settling into a seat across the aisle from him.

He frowned as she pulled out her mobile phone and searched for a number. "Don't you know it's rude to ignore someone to talk on the phone?"

"Not when it's business."

"What's business?"

She motioned between the two of them. "This trip." Waving the phone for a minute, she continued, "And this call."

Oh, no she didn't. "What kind of business call could you possibly be making on a Saturday morning?"

"I'm calling Vivian. It was too late to call her last night and I should let her know where we'll be. You didn't give me nearly enough time pack and get ready and call her this morning."

And I'm not about to give you a chance now, either. He eyed her stiff shoulders and the haughty tilt to her chin as she studied the screen. She wore her defiance like a uniform—one he wanted to remove inch by inch. "Don't, Ziara."

"Why not?"

"Seriously? What good is it going to do?"

"It just might preserve my job when all this is over," she said, those chocolate eyes finally meeting his head-on. "Or did you forget that someone else has a stake in this besides you?"

Ouch. He knew it, even when he wished he didn't. *Not everyone needs a high salary and trust fund to be successful.* She needed her job. If everything didn't work out, he'd help her find a new one.

Standing, he loomed over her, hearing the call to board blast from the speakers around them. "Still, I'm in charge on this trip. Remember?"

With a quick snatch, he grabbed her phone and stored it deep in the pocket of his khakis. Still within reach...barely.

"Give that back," she demanded, her voice shaking.

"No. But you are welcome to come get it, if you want."

The anger that exploded over her face didn't hide the hint of interest that surfaced. Enjoying a touch of satisfaction, he grabbed his carry-on and strolled across the waiting area to board the flight. The whole time he could feel her glare directly between his shoulder blades.

This would be a fun flight.

On the plane, she lowered into the seat next to him with exquisite care, her tense jaw signaling extreme displeasure. He really shouldn't be enjoying this so much.

"Give back my phone."

"No," he said, giving a little jiggle of his pocket. "Look at it this way—at least you'll have an excuse when she asks why you didn't call."

If he had to guess, he'd say he was seeing his assistant go supernova. Not a sound was made, but the air almost shook around her before she closed her eyes and drew in a deep breath. As they started to taxi, she took out a paperback and began to read. Clearly all avoidance tactics were in full effect now, probably for his own safety. He grinned. Biding his time was a talent he'd long ago acquired.

He allowed her to avoid him until they'd reached cruising

altitude. Then his nimble fingers plucked the book from hers before she knew what was coming.

"Hey," she protested. "Are you planning to make stealing a habit?"

"I don't know. Haven't you learned yet it's rude to ignore the person you're traveling with?"

She angled herself toward the window, leaving him with a devastating view of her elegant nose and full lips, not to mention thick lashes that added to the mystery of her eyes. "I didn't want you to feel you had to entertain me."

He handed back the book, murmuring, "I'll just bet you did."

She shot him a sharp look but tucked the book into her purse for safekeeping. Settling back in her seat, she folded her hands in her lap like the prim woman he suspected she wasn't. If she only knew what that contradiction did to him. Actually, it was probably a good thing she didn't. Ten thousand feet up in an airplane wasn't the ideal place for arousal.

"Aren't you curious about the designer we're going to see?"

She tilted her head toward him, the sun through the window highlighting the curve of her jaw and the smooth caramel skin of her neck. He bet she'd taste just as sweet.

"Okay," she said, drawing out the word. "I'll bite. Who is it?"

Sloan accepted a drink from the flight attendant. Passing Ziara one of the small glasses, he deliberately brushed his fingers along hers. Her quick retreat confirmed his suspicions. She wasn't as immune to him as she'd like. If he played his cards right on this trip, Ziara's loyalties to him would far outweigh any hold Vivian had on her.

"Patrick was my college roommate. He was a fashion design major while I stuck it out on the business track." He paused a moment at her considering look. "I immediately thought of him when I decided to do this project, but he turned me down."

"Then why are we on a plane to Las Vegas?"

"I'm going to change his mind."

* * *

Great. She wasn't on a flight to Las Vegas to meet their new designer but to court one. A reluctant one.

She shouldn't be surprised that Sloan wouldn't take no for an answer. Keeping that in mind in her own dealings with him would be smart. After all, hadn't he just shown her in graphic detail how opposed he was to a little phone call? If he thought she was going to go diving into his pants for her phone—or tell Vivian exactly where said phone had been—he was gravely mistaken.

Maybe she could dig into his plans before he realized what she was doing and shut her out completely.

"I don't know of any big wedding dress designers based in Vegas. Who does he work for?"

Sloan's smirk didn't answer any questions; it only created more. "You won't believe it until you see it."

She sighed in frustration. "What does that mean?"

He leaned toward her, his eyes meeting hers head-on. Her stomach jumped, but she told herself it was from turbulence.

"Ziara, we're on our way to Las Vegas. Relax and enjoy a little pleasure with your business."

Alarm skittered through Ziara when her mental walls didn't go up immediately. She actually wanted to give in to the attraction tempting her, but knew doing so would cost her all she'd worked so hard for, so she pulled back.

"I'm just here to work," she said, hoping she sounded like an old, repressive aunt. "What do you think it will take to convince this friend of yours to change his mind?"

He frowned, collapsing back in his seat. She couldn't help but admire the ease he seemed to feel in his body. "Probably something I'm not going to want to give."

"Why?"

"Because he knows me too well."

She angled toward him in her small seat. "So you must have been really close and stayed in touch all this time."

He shrugged. "We have similar interests."

What did that mean? Ziara wanted to pull her hair in frustration. Or better yet, shake Sloan until all the answers she wanted just tumbled out. His secretive, *I don't trust you* attitude was getting really old, really quick. If he couldn't trust her, that was his problem. Though she should probably be happy she wasn't dealing with a flirty, sexy boss, instead.

"Is there anything you'd like to do in Vegas?" Sloan asked out of the blue. "A show? Shopping?" His gaze slid over her, heating her flesh even through her sensible pantsuit. "Dance with a sexy stranger?"

From anyone else, the question would have seemed presumptuous and sleazy, but from Sloan it was, well, presumptuous and tempting. What would it be like to dance secure in his arms, to give herself up to his lead without having to worry where he'd take her? Without having to worry how he'd feel about her in the morning?

She'd never chance it. This time she leaned forward, meeting him head-on so there would be no mistakes. This tactic had worked time and again in the past. Attitude was everything, though the lock on her bedroom door had come in handy too.

She might be physically tempted like never before, but it wouldn't show. She wouldn't allow it.

"Let's get this straight," she said in a calm, nonthreatening sort of way. "I have no interest outside of helping you find your designer and launch the fall line. I'm here to do my job. Period."

Instead of backtracking or scrambling for excuses like all the men before him under her no-nonsense glare, Sloan simply watched her lips as she formed the words, his gaze tracing every curve. The urge to moisten them with a slip of her tongue grew strong.

A satisfied expression crossed his face, as if he'd stumbled upon a secret she hid deep inside. "We'll see," he said simply, then leaned back in his chair and closed his eyes, leaving her to stew in her amazement at his audacity.

We'll see. *We'll see?* He'd see nothing more than her hand making contact with his face if he tried to pull anything on her. She knew far too much about the ways of men and the lengths they'd go to have a woman. She'd seen every trick before; nothing impressed her now. They all ended up looking at you like trash once you gave in. She'd vowed a long time ago that she'd never endure that. Respect meant everything to her. If she couldn't have it romantically, she'd earn it through hard work and initiative in her career.

She never let herself down. That was the only thing she could count on.

Seven

Ziara kept reminding herself of that until the plane touched down late that afternoon. The Nevada heat drained her. Just walking from the airport to the taxi sparked a thirst that for once had nothing to do with Sloan.

They checked into the hotel with relative ease. The elegant suite, thankfully complete with two bedrooms with locking doors, offered an enticing view from Ziara's balcony. Despite her resolve to focus on work, Ziara couldn't deny the little tendrils of excitement spreading through her veins. Vegas was an animal all its own and it tempted her curiosity almost as much as Sloan and his mystery designer.

As the sunset crept over the horizon and lights sparked on, she didn't care about the reputation of Sin City; she just wanted to indulge in a little color and stimulation.

She tried to dig some information out of Sloan during dinner in their sitting area. Knowing his plans would grant her more control and distract her from Sloan's good looks. He'd changed into a lightweight tan suit that brought out the blond highlights in his thick hair. The blue dress shirt, with the top buttons undone, echoed the icy blue of his eyes. He projected an aura of sophisticated relaxation. She couldn't help but envy that cool attitude.

Distraction, that's what she needed. "What is the itinerary while we're here?"

Sloan didn't even look up from his filet mignon. "I'm not sure."

She stifled a sigh. "Do we have an appointment to meet with your friend?"

"I'm afraid not." He paused to chew a bite of crunchy fried potatoes.

How did he eat like that and still maintain those lean muscles without an ounce of extra flesh?

"This trip was a spur-of-the-moment decision."

Really? She could feel her frustration tightening the muscles along her neck. Hadn't he planned any part of this little jaunt? Planning was her modus operandi. Besides, if the designer refused to meet with Sloan, this entire trip would be a complete waste of time.

"So is there at least a plan of attack?"

Realizing her frustration was beginning to ooze through the cracks in her calm facade, she cringed. Maybe she should just concentrate on the juicy chicken Alfredo on her plate. Then she quit caring altogether as she noticed the shake in Sloan's shoulders.

Tilting her head, she caught a glimpse of his laughing mouth. She barely restrained the urge to kick his shin with her pointy dress pumps. Taking a deep breath, instead, she applied herself to her food in outward silence, but inside her mind was calling him every name in the book. And she knew quite a few more than people imagined.

Sloan must have decided he'd tested her type A personality quite enough, because he broke the silence. "I bought tickets for a show here tonight. Since we won't be able to catch up with Patrick until later, we might as well enjoy ourselves."

He studied her as if expecting a protest, but she decided to ease off the hall monitor bit for a little while. Heck, everyone

needed a day off. Including her. If he wanted to take her out—
strictly as her boss—then who was she to complain?

After finishing their meal, Sloan cleared everything to the
room service cart and rolled it outside the door. Ziara changed
into the only nonbusiness outfit she'd brought. The plain summer skirt and lack of a suit jacket evoked a sense of freedom
from her responsibilities. Paired with a light summer sweater,
she was ready to be entertained. The assessing look in Sloan's
eyes had her reluctantly standing a bit straighter.

Exiting the elevators, they crossed through the hotel lobby
toward the theater. Passing the opening to the casino, various
restaurants and shops, Ziara caught the excitement of tourists
and let herself slowly slip into the mood, just a little.

A burgundy-uniformed usher led them to seats close to the
front, slightly left of the center aisle. Sloan must have pulled
strings to get such good seats at the last minute. As the lights
lowered and the stage came alive, Ziara's breath caught in her
throat. She felt close enough to be part of the action, yet iso-
lated in the dark, alone, with only the warmth of Sloan's arm
next to hers anchoring her.

The show was a compilation of variety acts. As Sloan's
laughter rumbled in his chest at the comedian, Ziara let herself
join in. She held her breath, awed over the awesome acrobat-
ics and stunts in various sketches.

At one point Sloan stretched out his long legs, the brush
of material against the bare skin of her calf setting off goose
bumps. His gaze branded her like a heat-seeking missile, taking in her reactions to the various acts onstage, reminding her
to temper her laughter or excitement.

She thoroughly enjoyed the evening until the next-to-last
act. As a scantily clad woman gracefully crossed the stage and
burst into song, Ziara cringed in her seat.

She knew the song well—it had been one of her mother's fa-
vorites. The scene was from a musical about a prostitute who'd
found Mr. Right and hoped he'd look past her profession to the
woman within. As fellow "call girls" made their way onto the
stage to join in the chorus, Ziara shifted in her seat.

Like a neon sign right before her face, the scene reminded her of all she had to lose if she gave in to her attraction to Sloan. Her past and future colliding in one tempting, disastrous physical attraction. Each word of the song pounded at her temples, reawakening her anger and resolution.

She wasn't her mother and never would be. But she knew from experience that people, especially men, treated her differently when they found out about her childhood. Their attitudes changed. Their words changed. Above all, their eyes changed.

Vivian would definitely change if Ziara's past found the light of day.

Abruptly Sloan stood, grasping her hand to pull her to her feet, then guide her up the aisle to the muted lighting of the foyer. As he paused outside the auditorium doors, she turned to him, acutely conscious of his hand still wrapped around hers. She blinked, her vision adjusting to the faint light, bright after the darkness of the theater.

"What is it?" she asked, withdrawing slightly as he studied her with uncomfortable intensity. That gaze didn't miss much, and she felt as vulnerable as an open book right now.

"You seemed to have lost interest, so I thought it was time to go," Sloan said, a question in his voice.

She shifted, firmly drawing her hand from his grasp. "What makes you say that?"

Stupid! Her defensiveness would surely make him even more curious. Too bad she didn't have a real zipper in her mouth like she'd pretended to as a child, then she could zip her lips shut so nothing incriminating could leak out.

He stepped closer, as if to regain any ground lost by letting go of her hand. She checked the urge to retreat. "You kept wiggling. You seemed uncomfortable and weren't watching the stage despite the excellent performances."

He reached out and pushed an errant strand of hair back behind her ear. Her flesh tingled at the contact, speeding up her heartbeat.

"Was it the performance or the content?"

Now her heart pounded in her chest, drowning out any

sound around her. She made the mistake of meeting his gaze; those cool, steady eyes coaxing her to spill her secrets. But if he knew, knew what her mother had been, those eyes would change. They would glitter, hard as ice, as he condemned her just like her classmates and the townspeople of good ol' Macon, Georgia. Only this time, the life she'd built would be at stake, not just her heart.

"We've got somewhere to be," he said, turning away without waiting for an answer. Had he drawn his own conclusions?

As she followed him down several hallways, she pulled herself back into professional mode, sharp and on alert around Sloan's prying eyes.

Her first inkling that all was not as she suspected came when Sloan led her through a nondescript door that opened into a back corridor near the theater. After several minutes of walking, they came to a door marked Backstage with a doorman keeping a close eye on things. Sloan pulled something from his jacket pocket and the man waved him in.

Going through that door was like entering another dimension. Whereas earlier Ziara had been dazzled by the lights, sounds and effortless flow of the production, now she was amazed that such beauty came from such chaos.

Performers stood in groups chatting or rushing to and from who knows where. Stagehands attended to curtains, props and other mysterious tasks, sidestepping anyone or anything in their way. But it was nearly silent chaos, for the tone of the noise remained low and soft, ever aware of the audience and performance not too far away.

Sloan led her deeper into the backstage area, through rooms containing waiting performers. Here the noise level rose, protected from the stage by distance. Finally they came to a long, narrow room lined with dressing tables. Sloan didn't even blink at the number of women—very toned, well-built women—in various stages of undress, though several certainly noticed him.

He made a beeline to the far end of the room with Ziara cautiously following, awkward under the eyes tracking their progress. Finally Sloan stopped, moving slightly to one side so that Ziara came up even with him. Before them stood one of the performers, a showgirl decked out in a wisp of spandex and sequins. Ziara's gaze trailed down the outfit to catch sight of a man crouched behind the girl, one hand inside the bottom of her outfit and a needle and thread in the other. His spiky blond hair was just level with her rear end, as he leaned close to repair a seam.

"Ziara," Sloan said, "I'd like you to meet Patrick Vinalay, my roommate from college."

Ziara's heart stopped at the shock, then resumed beating again triple time.

This would definitely not go over well. Vivian would throw a true hissy fit if Sloan hired this man to design her wedding dresses. Ziara managed a sickly smile as Sloan introduced her to Patrick's assistant, who was standing nearby.

"Welcome to the drudgery behind the glamour," Patrick said, waving a hand around them at the glittering chaos.

"It's nice to meet you," she murmured, at a loss for anything else to say. Fortunately he turned to Sloan, relieving her of the need for small talk. Her brain couldn't form a coherent sentence; she was still shell-shocked by the bomb Sloan had dropped on her.

What had he been thinking, to offer a man with this background first chance to modernize their line? Patrick was probably great at what he did, but that was the problem. What bride wanted to look like a Vegas showgirl on her wedding day? Eternity Designs was known for its elegance, subtle beauty... not tacky sequins.

Patrick stood, dropping the needle and thread on a table behind him. "So what brings you to Vegas, Sloan? I guess if you brought your assistant, you aren't here for a little *wink-wink*." Patrick accompanied the words with the matching motion. Then his eyes widened. "Or are you?"

The sound of distress—all Ziara could manage—had both men turning toward her. Patrick quickly backtracked. "I'm just kidding! A little off-color college humor between buddies. I'll try to remember my audience in the future."

But the serious consideration she caught lurking in Sloan's gaze sent heat rushing to her face. And the knowledge that some physical recreation hadn't been far from her mind from the moment she'd laid eyes on Sloan Creighton.

Moving closer, he cupped a hand on Patrick's shoulder. "I'm actually here on business."

A knowing, exasperated look crossed Patrick's face. "This wouldn't be about the design position, would it?"

"Of course. Why else would I take time out of my busy schedule to come to Sin City?"

"Oh, how about the glamour? The excitement?"

"Do I look like I have time for all that?" Sloan asked without a change of expression.

Patrick prodded some more. "Sexy women and high-stakes gambling?"

As a waiting showgirl called to Patrick, Sloan laughed. "I don't need all that. I just need a designer."

Shaking his head, Patrick gestured toward the girl in front of him. "Look, I've got to get this done before she has to be onstage for the final number. We'll talk after the curtain falls. Now get out of here," he said with a stern look around the dressing room. "You're distracting the girls."

Patrick's assistant peeked around his boss's shoulder. "And the boys," he said, his tone flirty.

Ziara tensed, unsure how Sloan would feel about this turn of events, but he simply threw a look at Patrick.

"Don't bother," Patrick said. "He's not interested, much to the disappointment of many of my friends throughout the years."

He favored Ziara with another cheeky wink, then crouched behind the woman once more. Ziara pulled Sloan by his arm into a darkened, abandoned corner. "Have you totally lost your mind?" she asked, her tone surprisingly calm and steady, though she was shaking on the inside. Her controlled voice and out-of-control words prompted a laugh from Sloan.

Knowing by now that honesty was the best way to reach him, she continued, "Do you have a death wish? Because Vivian will certainly kill you if you try to bring a costume designer in to work on our wedding dress line."

Sloan's eyes narrowed, his back stiffening in a way that made her swallow, hard. "Our? If I don't step up now, before Bridal Boutique sees the fall designs, there won't be a business left to save. This isn't a game to me, Ziara."

He loomed closer, his broad shoulders inducing a feeling of claustrophobia in the dusty space, leaving her vulnerable to his size. "Since it isn't Vivian's reputation on the line, I don't give a damn what she thinks."

"I understand your urgency, just not your secrecy. This wild idea is exactly why you need someone to provide balance," Ziara said.

"For the record, I'm keeping it quiet because I don't want her shooting down a plan that has nothing to do with her. Understand?"

Ziara drew in a deep breath, choking a little on the dry, dusty air. She knew exactly what Sloan meant. Vivian would do everything in her power to stop this, even if it lost them the Bridal Boutique account. Reputation was everything to her, as Ziara well knew.

"I don't agree with this choice." Ziara waved a hand in Patrick's general direction. "I understand why you are trying so hard to fix this problem. But why him?"

"Because he knows what he's doing," Sloan said.

"That's right," Patrick said from over Sloan's right shoulder, making Ziara jump. "I do know what I'm doing. Besides a degree in fashion design, I know my way around a booty, as you can see." He quirked a grin. "That should come in handy designing lingerie."

Ziara's chest tightened, cutting off her breath for a moment. Sloan's body remained close enough that she could feel the half laugh, half groan he choked back, but when she looked up, his face was still.

Her heart knew this wasn't a joke. Vivian had sensed all

along that Sloan was holding something back, that he might try something crazy. She'd had good reason to be concerned, because this was big. A lingerie line, no matter how tastefully done, would shatter Eternity's conservative reputation forever.

"You're adding a lingerie line," she said with a soft undertone of conviction. "No wonder you've been… You certainly did have something to hide."

Sloan's chin jutted forward, his aggressive stance for once matching his personality. "Are you going to run to Vivian and tattle like a good little girl?"

"Vivian. Good God!" Patrick said with an exaggerated shiver. "If she's involved, that's just one more reason to turn you down. That woman could intimidate the Pope."

Sloan ignored him, his gaze locked with Ziara's. He reached out to once more trace her jawline, his fingers gently abrasive against her sensitive skin.

"Which will it be, Ziara? Friend or foe?"

Eight

Sloan watched as Ziara struggled not to fidget during brunch the next morning. He knew exactly what the problem was, but putting her out of her misery by laying out a plan for the day wouldn't be nearly as fun as his current torture tactics.

She bided her time through coffee, waffles, eggs, mimosas and filet mignon, until she looked like the words would burst through her locked lips at the slightest provocation. He waited just a minute more, but she beat him to it.

"Are we seeing Patrick today?"

"I'm not entirely sure of his plans. We'll have to play it by ear." He could see uncertainty roll over her like a bumpy log. Any minute now steam would come billowing out of her ears. How could it be more fun to torture this woman than it was to sleep with other women? How had he even reached the point where he would ask himself that question?

"So are you excited about the lingerie line?" Sloan asked, a grin finally breaking free.

"Look," she said, that disapproving librarian look making a reappearance. "This is not some kind of game like you seem to think it is. Start talking, or I'll be on the phone to Vivian in two minutes."

He felt his mouth drop open, unable to believe she would adopt his own overbearing approach. Yet aroused by it, just the same.

"I want to understand, Sloan. I really do. But lingerie? Please explain this to me."

He drew in a deep breath before starting. "It's all about marketability—" His hand shot up to stop her from interrupting. "Let me explain." He wiped his mouth with the cloth napkin, then tossed it onto his plate.

"Vivian is focused on making the least amount of change that she can to get by." Standing, he worked off his restless energy by pacing to the glass balcony doors. "Hell if I know why. But that's not how to run a profitable business that will remain stable for the foreseeable future."

He saw logical understanding in her eyes but not the spark of passion he hoped for. He found himself wanting her to understand, needing her to understand. "Modern designs are great. Any willing designer can make those changes." His pacing picked up speed. "But I want a whole new approach—something different, a big splash to make us stand out from the crowd."

Halting, he found himself across the room from her. She sat at the table, her hands folded loosely on the smooth black top. His mind filled with an image of her dressed in lace and pearls for her wedding day, the epitome of elegance.

He mused aloud. "Most women shopping for their weddings already associate Eternity Designs's brand with their big day. Why not expand their thinking to their wedding night, too?"

She shifted. Fear battled with a growing interest in her eyes.

Suddenly he stepped forward, approaching her at a slow stalk. Her throat worked as she swallowed hard. He circled around, pausing behind her. The sweet scent of vanilla swirled in the air. Her personal scent. His gaze branded her at the vulnerable base of her neck.

"Think about it, Ziara—" Just like he was. "There you are,

preparing to put on the dress of your dreams. What do you wear underneath it?"

Leaning forward, he caged her in with an arm on each side. The glimpse of her face lured him to push her further. "Do you want to squeeze into a too-tight piece of Lycra? Itchy lace? Ugly beige?"

Her brows drew together over her now-closed eyes. Following his body's instincts, he lowered his voice, hoping to evoke the images in her mind.

"Or would you rather stand before the mirror in something just as sexy and beautiful as your dress, confident that your husband-to-be will be just as happy when your dress comes off as when he sees you walking down that aisle?"

He shifted closer, his own mind exploding with visions of her in flaming red satin, dark purple silk and then nothing at all. He barely covered a groan.

"Think about a silky smooth body shaper trimmed in soft lace, the same cream color as the dress. No ugly stitching and oxygen-stealing constriction. A strapless bra the perfect shape for your dress's neckline, with smooth, shaped cups and peek-aboo netting."

A grimace twisted her lips.

"What was that?" he whispered, speaking very close to her right ear. Shivers raced across her skin.

"Nothing," she said, but her voice choked on its way out.

"Ah, methinks the lady has a small problem with sensual…"

Her breath paused just as he did.

"…clothes."

With a whoosh, she started to breathe again. *Dangerous territory,* his mind whispered. She wasn't just resisting because of Vivian—she shied away because something was making her uneasy. Why was a woman whose home was filled with color and spice afraid of the same when she was in his presence?

"You know what?" he asked, backing away as a plan took shape in his brain.

He circled around to stand beside her. Though what came next would probably be the last thing on her agenda, he refused to ask. Only demand. He wanted to know *why*. "We'll perform a little experiment."

"Experiment?" Her high-pitched squeak sent a hot flush through him.

"Yep, time for a field trip." He grabbed her hand, urging her to her feet when she would have resisted. "Let's go."

Oh, this situation had just escalated from bad idea to worse.

The elevator offered her no protection from his probing gaze. She shifted from foot to foot, as if she was a naughty schoolgirl on her way to the principal's office.

He took advantage of their isolation to push her a little further. "Why are you so judgmental of the lingerie idea? Is it the notion of change or the lingerie itself?"

She kept her gaze resolutely fixed on the numbers marking their downward journey. "I'm simply worried about my job," she said. "Vivian would not appreciate having Eternity Designs associated with…that…"

"Ah, so it's the lingerie itself."

"What?" she asked with a gasp, only to look at him and catch his satisfied grin. "I did not say that."

The grin widened. "You didn't have to."

He didn't speak again, but instead let the silence build until she rushed to fill it. "I think it's just, you know." Her hand gestured toward her body in an awkward jerk.

"I don't know. What?" He drew the word out.

"It just seems dirty."

"Seen a lot of it, have you?"

Ziara gave a simple shrug of her shoulders, but the red that rushed up her chest and into her cheeks told a whole different story. And had him licking his lips.

"Obviously not," he said as the elevator doors slid open on the ground floor. "It's time for your education."

Ziara struggled not to choke on her hot embarrassment as she stood beside Sloan. Not even her Indian heritage could hide this blush.

Around my mom's house, I saw it all the time. But she wasn't about to detail her mother's favorite business wear. That woman had never made a secret of what she did for a living—at home or away from it.

Ziara followed Sloan at a trot as he strode through the bustling indoor avenues that traversed the ground floor of their hotel. At first she suspected they were heading for the casino floor with its scantily clad waitresses or even another show. Instead, they silently traveled quite a distance to an indoor promenade fashioned as a replica of a high-end Parisian shopping district lined with quaint, expensive little shops.

Now they stood facing one and she was deathly afraid of what he would demand next.

A lingerie store.

If he expected her to tour a place like that with him at her side, the heat might rise to explosive temperatures. Tremors radiated from her thighs to her calves. It could have been the fast pace of the walk, but she suspected it was dread of what loomed on her horizon.

Sloan made no immediate demands. Instead, he planted his feet, crossed his arms over his chest and studied the delicate ironwork framing the front windows. "What do you see, Ziara?"

The stuff of my nightmares. She settled for, "A store."

The sound grumbling low in his throat could have been disapproval...or a threat. "Look closer. Describe it to me."

Taking a deep breath, she brought her focus to the windows.

The wince was involuntary, a force of habit as she glimpsed the barely there bra-and-panty sets, the sheer teddies, the lace-only gowns. So she turned her attention to the framework—aged wrought iron in fancy curlicues decorating the windows as if they were paintings—

"Out loud," Sloan said, breaking into her thoughts. His voice remained soft, but there was no mistaking the steel undertone. "Describe it to me, Ziara."

Swallowing anger at his high-handedness, she said, "The windows remind me of pictures, feminine and delicate. The pink-and-brown decor is also feminine, like candy and chocolate, but classy, like a sophisticated chocolatier."

"Very good. Go on."

She let her eyes slip to the lingerie, then quickly pulled back. "I don't know. It's underwear." Or outerwear, depending on the woman.

Silence engulfed them in the midst of the eddying crowd. As the seconds ticked by, Ziara's internal tension wound tighter and tighter. Whatever this test was, she was obviously failing.

"Ziara, I want you to go inside."

Yikes.

"Go inside and see for yourself. And I mean really look. Lingerie does not have to be slutty."

She scoffed. "Tell that to—" Her teeth clamped shut.

"To who?" he asked, his voice barely loud enough to be heard above the noise from the crowds.

The shake of her head was sharp, a reflection of the anger building inside of her. She had no idea where it came from or why it filled her so quickly. But it had to stop. *She* had to stop. The cracks would get too wide and then she'd never be able to repair them.

"I can't do this, Sloan." Turning on her heel, she was stopped by two strong hands with the softest of holds on her upper arms.

"Wait, Ziara," he said, his voice once more soft, speaking into her ear just as he had in the privacy of their suite. Here, it was just as intimate. "You can do this. I know you can. You simply have to trust me."

"You don't know," she whispered, not even sure he could hear her.

"Whatever it is, I want you to lock it away."

She thought she had, but not well enough.

"Lock it away and go in with fresh eyes. Use those gorgeously sensitive fingers to explore, to discover. Trust me."

If only I could... But she couldn't say that out loud, so she simply nodded her head. His hands slid down her arms, then defected to her waist, leaving tingles of awareness in their wake. Then he turned her to once again face the storefront. "Go in."

She was halfway to the door when the fear took hold of her. Glancing over her shoulder, her eyes met his. Without a word, he urged her forward. Without a word, she followed his command.

The fabrics were beautiful, tempting her to touch, to stroke, to explore the texture and feel. But each time she reached out, she could sense Sloan tracking her progress from display to display. His gaze blanketed her in warmth, strength. She could almost feel him surrounding her, pushing her, enticing her.

A nightgown, pale gray and silky smooth, slid over her fingertips. She could imagine it against her skin, caressing her hips, the sensitive tips of her breasts. Sloan's gaze had her wondering if he imagined her in the silvery fabric, too.

Somehow the nightie and a matching robe found their way into her hands. A spot of the same silvery gray color caught her eye from a nearby table. Panties had always been utilitarian for her. Waistband and shape were chosen for comfort.

But with the first stroke she imagined wearing them for Sloan's hot gaze. She couldn't begin to see herself in a thong, but the dramatic curve of the high-cut briefs would line the edges of her backside with sheer lace. The phantom feel of his fingers tracing the edges brought a shiver along her spine, daring her to look over her shoulder through the outer windows.

She couldn't, wouldn't, but she scooped several colors into her hands and moved to the register before she could think any more about it. All the while, Sloan's presence called to her from just outside the door. His tracking gaze should have induced embarrassment. Instead, every glimpse of him through those wide windows brought the warm reminder of comfort, encouragement and, yes, trust. Along with a desire to be a woman she was not.

Without him she'd have never even spared this store a glance.

Her rush out the door slowed as she noticed a corner set off from the rest of the store. A quick glance made her think, *Wedding night,* prompting her to pause, to wonder.

A younger woman held up a thigh-length confection of cream satin, lace and pearls. Her companion, who was old enough to be her mother and probably was, smiled, whispering something that encouraged a nod from the daughter. They walked toward the dressing rooms, leaving Ziara watching them with loneliness creeping into her heart.

And confusion.

At first she'd been convinced Sloan was out of his mind. But maybe, just maybe, he was on the right track.

Getting married was a precious vow. She knew that even though she'd never witnessed or wanted that happily ever after herself. What if Sloan could extend the traditions of Eternity Designs to the private celebrations of marriage and not just the public ones?

For an instant the desire to experience a love deep enough for that kind of commitment overwhelmed her, settling at the pit of her stomach in a tide of need. She'd been alone so long, depending only on herself, the only person she could trust. What would it be like to give in to those feelings of overwhelming attraction, to trust someone to understand your needs rather than judge you for them?

She shook her head. With unerring accuracy, she turned to the windows and met Sloan's bright blue gaze once more. Deliberately lowering her lashes, she forced her thoughts to the lasting image of the mother's smile. She would never experience the feminine bond of shopping for her wedding night. Even though her mother wasn't dead, shopping for lingerie with a prostitute was a whole different experience from what she'd just witnessed. She knew. She'd lived it.

Nine

Following Sloan back into the cool air-conditioning of the hotel suite, Ziara noticed the sweat coating her neck and scalp as she took her purchases to her room. A pounding headache—whether from the building tension or lingering emotions—throbbed in her temples and down along her jaw. A few minutes alone, that's all she needed. Time away from Sloan's probing gaze and questioning looks.

He'd watched her closely as she returned to him on the promenade, his eyes flicking between her face and the bag in her hands. That's when the arousal had hit her, this time piercing and sharp. Almost painful. It would be a long time before she forgot that particular sensation.

In the bathroom she pulled the pins from her hair, allowing the heavy weight to fall below her shoulders. She ran a quick brush through the mass. Sometimes just letting it down was enough to ease her tension headaches.

Walking into her bedroom, she moved to close her door so she could rest for a while, but the phone rang. Not hearing any sound in the suite outside, she crossed to the extension beside her bed, stretching her neck from side to side as she went. Taking a deep breath, she answered.

"Hello?"

"Ziara?" Vivian's voice rang in her ear, stealing her breath for a moment. A wealth of suspicion and condemnation resided in that one word.

"Yes, Vivian?"

"Would you like to explain to me what you are doing in Sloan's hotel room?"

For a moment, Ziara's head swirled. Her own concerns mixed with remembered insults and insinuations from the past. She forced herself to breathe, remembering Vivian knew nothing about her past. And never would if she had anything to say about it.

"Actually," Ziara said, grateful her voice came out calm and even, "I'm in my own room. Sloan booked us into a suite so we'd have a common area for working."

Vivian didn't answer immediately, as if pondering Ziara's explanation. This time her voice was a little less tight. "Good. I'd hate to see your reputation compromised by Sloan's charm."

Words rushed to Ziara's lips in her own defense, but she held them back. They would sound like token protests. Besides, hadn't she been tempted? Like Eve by the snake.

"Thank you for your concern," she murmured.

"Ziara, why didn't you contact me about this trip? Why didn't you keep me informed as I instructed?"

Because my phone was resting a little too close to your stepson's privates for me to comfortably make a phone call.

She could have made the phone call after getting to the hotel, but by that time she'd convinced herself that Monday was soon enough to let Vivian know.

Oh, wouldn't that go over well? She decided on a half-truth. "By the time I realized we were going, it was too late to call. I mistakenly thought I could inform you of everything when I returned."

Maybe her growing attraction for Sloan was corroding the responsible part of her brain, but she just hadn't been able to call without his consent. Her mind had justified the need for more information, more…something.

Now she had more of the facts, and she was starting to see Sloan's point of view. Scary, but holding back seemed to be the right plan. For now. Besides, Vivian would faint dead away if she knew who Sloan was here to see.

"I'm truly sorry, Vivian." She used her most placating tone, the one reserved for unhappy clients. "I had to rush to be ready for an early flight Saturday morning."

There wasn't any need to tell her Sloan had come to her house. Vivian would find that move totally unprofessional.

"I see. That does sound like a stunt he would pull. We all know he wants me kept in the dark as long as possible."

Thankfully, that statement was totally true.

"Well, on a personal level, let me warn you, if I may." Vivian's tone didn't sound like a gentle warning. More like a harsh command. "Be careful. You don't want to end up like all the rest of Sloan's assistants, now do you?"

"What do you mean?"

"He has a history of going through them like Kleenex. Oh, he says the feelings, the misconceptions are all their faults. But I know that they are drawn in by his charm, and when he's used them, he discards them with little thought."

Aren't you glad that attitude didn't run in the family? Ziara knew the thought was petty, but Vivian's comments disturbed her on many levels. She didn't want to believe, but then again, what if Vivian spoke the truth? Didn't Sloan flirt and tease her? Hadn't he just taken her to a lingerie store?

Ziara's goal for her entire adult life had been an honorable career. She wanted an employer who respected her for who she was, what she was capable of, not a series of dirty, no-meaning encounters that would put her back in the ugliness of her childhood. Especially if she did it with her boss.

"I promise to keep that in mind."

"Good. I'm only trying to look out for you," Vivian said in an overly sweet tone. "As your mentor, and someone who knows Sloan very well, I don't want to see you get hurt."

"I understand, Vivian."

Even as she spoke, Ziara could feel guilt creeping in. Vivian had done so much for her. Her loyalties toward the woman who had nurtured her career and Eternity Designs were being ripped apart, piece by piece, by her growing attraction to Sloan, reinforcing the doubt Vivian planted in her mind.

"Now," Vivian's voice intruded, "I assume you've gone to Las Vegas to court a designer, though why he'd be there I have no clue. And why we need one is lost on me."

Yet another topic fraught with minefields. "Yes, Sloan is looking into a designer here, but I don't think anything definitive has been decided."

"Hmm, does he look any good? What do you think of his work?"

Well, if you are into tassels and sequins... "Actually I haven't had the chance to see any of his work yet," she said, hiding behind another little lie. Because if Vivian knew Sloan wanted a costume designer, she'd be on the first plane headed anywhere near Las Vegas. Ziara wasn't ready for that—yet. "I've only briefly met him. I think Sloan is hoping for a more formal meeting tonight."

She could hear the *tap, tap, tap* of Vivian's gold pen against her desk. That habit always indicated she was thinking hard.

"Well, I guess it wouldn't do any good to tell him I called. Is there anything else you think I need to know?"

Ziara's stomach tightened. Her legs went shaky. This was a big step, putting her own career on the line. But some small niggle in the pit of her stomach said Sloan might be on to something with this lingerie idea. He certainly wasn't going to get a lot of cooperation from Robert. She had to know for sure before she could decide where her *company* loyalty lay.

"No. Right now there's nothing more to tell."

Another tension-filled pause. Did Vivian suspect she knew more than she was letting on? "Very well. Keep me informed."

Ziara stifled a sigh and said simply, "Yes, ma'am."

After disconnecting, Ziara sank to the bed, her wobbly knees no longer able to support her traitorous stand.

Had she just made an irrevocable decision based on her physical response to the wrong man, a man who could never be more than her boss, instead of practical career considerations? She hoped not, because if Vivian learned she'd hid something so important from her, her career with Eternity Designs would be over.

Was making the fall line a success more important than her own need for security? The answers weren't so clear-cut anymore—no matter who ended up controlling the company. Hopefully, Vivian would never know at what point Ziara discovered the truth.

Like any dangerous pilgrimage, moving forward was the only option. She had to see where Sloan was heading with what she now knew were two new lines. Rising to her feet, she straightened her clothes, then turned toward the door, all thoughts of a nap now abolished from her mind.

Sloan stood in the doorway.

Ziara froze, absorbing his powerful presence, though he leaned casually against the doorframe with his arms crossed over his chest. His face had softened into a slight smile, but his eyes tracked her every move.

The contrast threw her off once more. On the outside he appeared approachable, carefree and happy, but those intense blue eyes alerted her to the hunter within. Pushing away from the frame, he stalked toward her, the tired lines on his face becoming faintly visible. This quest was wearing on him, as well. Her fingers itched to trace the weariness with her fingertips, soothing it away like she would a wrinkle out of fabric, but she forced her hands to remain still.

Stopping so close that a deep breath would bring his chest into contact with hers, he slid his hands into her hair and covered her lips with his own.

Ziara's widened eyes closed as the explosion of sensation from her lips connected with the feel of his hands in the tumble of her hair. He kneaded her scalp as if to massage away the tension hiding there, and she melted into his embrace. Reason and logic disappeared. He could do whatever he wanted. *Just don't stop touching me.*

Never one to do things by half measures, Sloan's tongue plunged through her parted lips, sweeping across her own, igniting a flash of longing through her body. Long after the last of her intelligence had leaked from her brain, he pulled back a fraction. His hands remained anchored in her hair, his minty breath fanning across her face.

Forcing her heavy lids upward, her eyes met his. "What was that for?" she asked, embarrassed by the husky whisper of her voice.

His hands tightened against her head for a moment as if to draw her forward for another kiss but, instead, he spoke. "For keeping my secrets."

They stood immobile for long minutes, afraid to move and bring reality back into their fragile peace. Ziara had never experienced anything like their kiss. Everything before had been a simple match set to flame, but this time fireworks exploded.

She needed to back away, but she didn't.

Slowly his hands drew the silky weight of her hair forward and over her shoulders. "Beautiful," he whispered, though his eyes never left hers.

An urge unlike any she'd ever experienced swept through her. No previous desire, no previous need felt real compared to the intensity of this moment. With no thought, she leaned forward, eager to taste his kiss once more. He didn't back away.

Until a knock sounded on the door.

Sloan escaped to the outer room, leaving Ziara behind. One deep breath followed another. If he could just get his head in gear and think this through, he'd make the right choice. When he opened the door, a courier brought in a simple white box, fairly long and thick in size, tied with a deep purple bow.

Sloan closed the door and turned to catch sight of Ziara standing in her bedroom doorway. She hugged herself loosely across her middle, warning him that awkwardness had set in. Good thing he had something to break the ice.

He drew in another deep breath, willing his heart to stop racing. His response to her was unbelievably strong. "You have a delivery," he said.

"Me?"

As she walked to the table, he noted her hair swinging midway down her back. His hands itched to bury themselves in the dark, silky fullness again. He'd always suspected her hair would be extravagant when set free from the constraint of that bun thing, but the sight and feel of it surpassed his tantalizing dreams.

He watched her delicately untie the bow, her care and precision not surprising him. But her restraint had a different quality to it, something more than just her normal reserve.

He studied her movements. The contained excitement on her face, the slight parting of her lips. Did she ever receive surprises? Was there no one in her life to offer those happy moments, big or small? With an unexpected spike of jealousy, he hoped there wasn't another man. He'd seen no evidence of anyone at her house.

Was her family the reason she'd closed herself off from the sensual parts of life? Had someone hurt her, damaged her?

She lifted the lid slowly, then pushed aside the tissue covering the contents. Her eyes widened, that sweet mouth opening in a silent O. She didn't remove whatever was inside, simply caressed it with exploring fingertips just as he'd seen her do with the lingerie and design fabrics.

Before those luscious strokes could completely shatter his control, Sloan walked forward to peer into the box himself. At first all he could see were layers upon layers of sheer, brightly colored fabric before he realized an expensive dress lay inside.

Sloan's suspicions were confirmed when Ziara pulled out the card tucked among the golden tissue.

"Patrick. But why?" she asked, turning to face him, though one hand remained resting amid the folds of the dress.

He opened the note. "We're invited to a party Patrick is hosting tonight. He wants you to wear this," he said, handing the paper over for her to read. His earlier jealousy settled like a lead brick in his stomach because Sloan himself hadn't been the one to make her eyes light up like stars.

She gazed back into the box but still didn't lift the dress. "I can't believe he did that." She looked at Sloan, a frown drawing those elegantly arched brows together. "Is this appropriate? I don't want to give the wrong impression."

"You worry too much. Of course it's okay to accept a gift. I'd say it's a sign we're headed in the right direction." Reaching in, he found the straps and lifted the dress, shaking it out to its full length. "Exquisite," he murmured.

Patrick's mind must have run along similar lines as Sloan's. The vibrant, flaming colors would be a stunning complement to Ziara's dark caramel skin and black hair. The soft, handkerchief layers of the skirt echoed her femininity, as did the cut pieces attached to the form-revealing bodice. His lips pressed together as he slipped into creative mode.

"I don't think I can wear this."

Sloan surfaced from his thoughts at the sound of Ziara's shaky voice. "Of course you can. This dress was made for you."

She shook her head, those soft waves of hair framing her face. "No, I can't. I'd feel too exposed."

Exposed? The dress did have only single straps across the shoulders, though they were thicker than spaghetti straps. The scoop of the neckline would reveal a little bit of cleavage, leaving her chest and arms bare. His mouth watered at the thought of all that delectable skin on display for his starving imagination.

He eyed the jacket she was wearing—her standard office fare. He remembered the T-shirt with its three-quarter-length sleeves that she wore in the middle of a hot Southern summer. Maybe there was more to her clothing than just an overblown sense of professionalism. If she was going to be stubborn about this—a grim smile slipped out—he had the perfect ammo for fighting back.

"Don't be stupid. You're wearing it."

"No." Her arms folded around her waist as if to anchor her clothes. Did she think he would strip her naked to force her to wear it? The tightening in his groin reminded him his thoughts were moving into dangerous territory.

He pulled back immediately, but pushing *her* out of her comfort zone would be good for her. The sensuous, open woman he'd glimpsed at her house needed releasing. If he benefited at the same time, all the better.

He tossed the dress toward the box, crowding forward to tower over her. "You don't get it, do you?" He connected his gaze with hers, insuring he had her full attention. This wasn't about business for him…his descent from lofty goals was gaining speed. But business was what she understood, so that's the reasoning he'd use.

"I want Patrick as my designer, and I'll do whatever I have to for him to agree. So if he sent a garbage bag with holes for the head and arms, you would be wearing that."

Her back stiffened and those lush lips thinned. Still he drove his point home. "We'll do whatever Patrick wants. Don't forget who's the boss around here."

Her eyes narrowed to a glare, her softly pointed chin edging up a notch.

"Now," he said, before he could give in to the temptation to kiss her pretty pout away, "go hang the dress up. We've got a party to get ready for."

"What are you talking about?" she asked. "The party isn't until eight tonight, and it's just now three."

God, her anger made her that much more beautiful and awoke an urge to channel it into a more mutually beneficial emotion.

"Trust me," he said. "We'll make every minute count."

Ten

Ziara's knees developed a tremor as she stared at herself in the mirror, making her unsteady on high-heeled gold sandals.

Sloan had instructed the hairdresser to leave her hair down, though she'd tucked one side up with a comb behind Ziara's ear. The orange, red and purple swirls of the dress and glint of gold threads hinted at a gypsy look, overlaid with Moroccan belly dancer.

The movement of the dress was reminiscent of veils, which emphasized the impression, along with her muted Indian heritage. Her skin seemed darker, more exotic. Her eyes more mysterious and shadowed. Her bearing more regal, like a princess tucked away in a harem—sensual, yet above approach.

The tremors grew, taking on a life of their own. Reminding herself that as Sloan's date, she didn't have to worry about anyone harassing her, she forced herself to walk to the door. But then, Sloan couldn't protect her from her own weaknesses, could he?

When she finally found the courage to leave her room, Sloan waited near the glass balcony doors. He turned to face her, his body a long, lean silhouette against the glittering backdrop of the city, whiskey tumbler in hand. An ache bloomed within her, a desire to meet him as an equal—strong, passionate and confident instead of closed off and broken.

He moved slowly into the light as he drank from the tumbler. His tongue slid across his lips, catching the last trace of amber alcohol. She followed the movement with her eyes, wishing she could lick the same path. He watched her, his light eyes sparking with desire as his gaze devoured the length of her body. These two days with him had attuned her to a whole level of herself she'd never known.

She stepped forward, conscious of the skirt, sheer from right above her knee down to the handkerchief points. Fear or revulsion should have set in, but neither did. Just a need to feel the heat of his mouth once again covering hers, her pulse pounding throughout the secret places of her body.

He stopped only inches away, forcing her to look up to see his face. The smooth line of his jaw, the taut muscles along his neck worked as he swallowed, making her own mouth water. But he didn't dip his head to indulge; instead, his eyes narrowed as a sexy grin spread across his full lips.

"I knew Patrick was the right designer for the job. He certainly knows what he's doing. This dress makes you look like magic."

His praise prompted her to stand a little straighter, ache to move a little closer, so she pulled back.

After clearing his throat, he said, "There was something else in the box."

"More?" She gestured to herself. "This is way too generous."

Sloan shrugged, his strong shoulders rippling under the slippery thin material of his button-down shirt. The blue made his eyes even more electric. Reaching into the pocket of his usual khaki pants, he pulled out a glittering length of golden circles. "He's a designer," Sloan said. "They want the look to be complete."

Ziara's mouth drained of moisture. Anxiety pounded at the

base of her throat, even though logic told her there wasn't any need for nerves. Then Sloan moved to put the chain around her throat.

"No." The force in her voice wasn't necessary, but she couldn't control it. Moderating a little, she continued, "No, please. I don't really like jewelry. It makes me uncomfortable."

"Why?" he asked with a frown.

Knowing any protest would just give him an opportunity to argue, she turned away. Moving to the balcony door of the suite, she escaped into the hallway with quick steps.

The limousine took them to a modest estate a short distance from the Strip. Ziara stepped out into night air that carried the tinkling sound of a center courtyard fountain. Through the open veranda windows drifted a soft rock song. The melody sounded vaguely familiar.

Sloan slipped up next to her, then tucked her hand into the crook of his arm. The gesture was a bit old-fashioned, part possessive, part protective. Despite her usual "no touching" rule, this calmed her nerves as they made their way up the stone steps.

They hadn't moved ten feet from the car before Patrick appeared through one of the arched doorways. The open floor plan of the house allowed glimpses of the adjoining rooms through the repeated arches.

"Ziara, you look exquisite," Patrick said, inspecting his creation and her in it. "Of course, I knew you would." Though his gaze lingered at her bare throat, he didn't mention the jewelry.

She smiled. "Thank you. And thank you for sending the dress." She fingered the skirt with her free hand, glancing down at the flaming swirl of material. "It's so beautiful."

Having stood silent long enough, Sloan said, "I knew you had talent, but this proves it. I'm tempted to up my offer."

Patrick frowned. "Sloan, no business. This is a party. Don't you remember how to have fun?" He pulled Ziara gently into his own grasp. "Let's mingle and meet about a hundred of my closest friends."

Ziara laughed, surprised the sound floated from her so

freely. The loosening of her control was almost a physical sensation.

Then she simply let herself follow Patrick's lead. He took them from group to group, making introductions. He didn't mention Ziara's status as Sloan's assistant. Her instinct was to correct him the first time, but something stopped her at the last minute. She didn't want to be that person right now, which was both scary and exhilarating.

Would the universe fall apart if she loosened up for just this one night?

They finally settled in with a small group of Patrick's theater buddies, one or two of whom had also known Sloan since college. After a period of catching up, one of the men turned to her. "And what do you do, Ziara?"

Unsure how much she should reveal, she answered, "I'm an executive assistant in training at a wedding gown design firm."

"Hey, Sloan, doesn't your family own one of those?" one of the men asked.

"Yep."

"Which is why I'm in training—to keep him on track," she said, unable to resist teasing.

Everyone chuckled. Before Sloan could make a snappy reply, Patrick stepped into the gap between them. "Could I borrow my buddies here for a few minutes? There's something I think they'd like to see."

Ziara nodded, smiling as the men stepped away. The women around her chatted about the wedding dress industry, distracting her from a sudden sense of vulnerability. With a deep breath, she remembered she could take care of herself. She'd been doing it every day since a very early age.

After chatting for a while, she excused herself to hunt down a drink. Despite the variety of alcohol at the bar, the parched Nevada air had put Ziara in desperate need of plain old water. When the waiter gave her the bottle, she opened it gratefully. The chilly liquid soothed her dry throat.

Someone bumped into her from behind, hard. Grimacing as

cold water splashed across her bodice, she tightened her grip on her drink and spun around.

"I'm sorry," said a man in a navy suit with a loosened tie, the top three buttons of his shirt undone. His gaze wavered and he took precise care in pronouncing his words. He was obviously drunk but trying to hide it.

"No harm done," she said, brushing at the water spots darkening her dress. She replaced the lid on her bottle for good measure. "It's just water. It'll dry."

He stared at her a moment before a pseudo-charming smile tightened his loose lips. "That's nice."

Her tension mounted as he closed the gap between them. She told herself he wouldn't attempt anything in a room full of people, but she'd seen enough drunks to know they were unpredictable.

"You're really pretty," he said, only slurring the words a little. His slight adjustment to his tie and straightening of his shoulders reinforced his attempt at being suave. It wasn't working for her.

"Thank you." She moved back a few steps before forcing herself to stop. *Stand your ground.*

"I think such beauty deserves a kiss." As the man advanced, Ziara held up her hands to maintain distance between them. Her water bottle dropped to the floor.

"Stop right there," she said, remembered panic adding force to her words. "I'm not interested, so you can just back away."

He paused. "What do you mean, not interested? I bet you're just saying that. Women who look like you are always interested."

His assumption punctured her normally impenetrable armor. Her arms wavered long enough for him to slip through. Grabbing her, he dragged her body closer. "I'll just have a taste of the goods for sale."

If his earlier words were a pinprick, these were a knife to the heart. The pain that lanced through her provided the strength to slam her foot down on his toes as he leaned forward to touch his lips to hers. Then she shoved him back, straight into Patrick's chest.

Sloan's friend surveyed the situation with wide eyes behind his designer wire-rimmed glasses. Sliding an arm around the man's shoulders, he said, "Come on, Michael. Let's get you into a taxi before my friend here decides to find the nearest meat grinder."

As Patrick led the drunk away, Sloan moved close to study her but kept his hands to himself. Her contrary body protested, aching for his touch.

"Are you okay?" he asked, his face tight.

"I'm fine," she said, struggling to control the sudden shake in her voice. She reached down for her water bottle. "No big deal."

He leaned forward until his eyes were level with hers. "Really? Because I don't think that guy's foot would agree with you."

A glance in that direction showed Patrick and the drunk had disappeared. "I'm sorry I made a scene at Patrick's party. I'll certainly apologize and smooth things over when he returns."

Sloan clasped her wrist, using it to guide her to a secluded corner. "I don't give a damn about any scene. That guy's lucky I didn't coldcock him. I'm kind of jealous that you handled it without me."

Though his mouth remained serious, his eyes smiled into hers. She was never so glad to see the crinkles along the sides.

"Well, a woman has to do what a woman has to do. This is the twenty-first century, you know."

"Does that mean I can't lead while we dance?" They shared a smile, then he bent close to her ear, his breath ruffling her hair. "I have the odd compulsion to throw a blanket over you. But I doubt you need me for protection."

She shivered, afraid of her sudden yearning for connection. Her body felt as if it was attached to an electric pulse. She'd never had this reaction to the few lovers she'd previously accepted, men she'd chosen very carefully for their safe auras.

The two who'd made it to the sexual stage hadn't been worth a repeat performance.

She had an inkling being with Sloan would be the performance of her life.

"Let's dance," he said in a husky whisper.

She stiffened, trying to pull back as he led her through the crowded rooms to the patio. "I don't think that's a good idea, Sloan. I've never danced before."

He paused. "Never?"

She shook her head.

"Not on a date?"

"No."

"Not even at a school dance?"

She shook her head again, not about to tell him she'd gone extra lengths to stay away from the guys around her school. Her mother's reputation wasn't a secret in her small hometown. Ziara had been harassed on more than one occasion by boys and girls alike—boys who expected something from her, girls who judged her for the same reason.

Sloan's trademark sexy grin slid into place, softening his face and sparking in those intent eyes. "Then I'll be the first."

They stepped onto the back patio, an oasis in the desert. Framed by potted and hanging plants, the stone mosaic floor created texture and color. Soft lighting from outdoor torches combined with the stars overhead, giving the feel of vast open space despite the others dancing and talking around them.

As a slow song floated on the air, Sloan chuckled. "Great. This will be an easy start."

With trepidation, Ziara let him pull her into his arms. Her fears—of giving in, of him seeing how she reacted and completely humiliating herself—kept her stiff. But when he settled her chest against his, their bodies in complete alignment, her muscles relaxed without her permission.

Her body openly rejoiced in Sloan's nearness, letting the earlier encounter fade from memory. The nervous shivers radiating from deep inside were chased away by his proximity—heat, height and a touch of humor.

FREE Merchandise is 'in the Cards' for you!

Dear Reader,

We're giving away FREE MERCHANDISE!

Seriously, we'd like to reward you for reading this novel by giving you **FREE MERCHANDISE** worth over $20. And no purchase is necessary!

You see the Jack of Hearts sticker above? Paste that sticker in the box on the Free Merchandise Voucher inside. Return the Voucher promptly...and we'll send you valuable Free Merchandise!

Thanks again for reading one of our novels—and enjoy your Free Merchandise with our compliments!

Pam Powers

Pam Powers

P.S. Look inside to see what Free Merchandise is **"in the cards"** for you!

HD-FM-08/13

W e'd like to send you two free books

to introduce you to the Harlequin Desire® series. These books are worth over $10, but they are yours to keep absolutely FREE! We'll even send you 2 wonderful surprise gifts. You can't lose!

REMEMBER: Your Free Merchandise, consisting of **2 Free Books** and **2 Free Gifts**, is worth over $20.00! No purchase is necessary, so please send for your Free Merchandise today.

YOUR FREE MERCHANDISE INCLUDES...

2 FREE Harlequin Desire® Books
AND 2 FREE Mystery Gifts

FREE MERCHANDISE VOUCHER

**2 FREE
BOOKS**
and
**2 FREE
GIFTS**

Please send my Free Merchandise, consisting of
2 Free Books and **2 Free Mystery Gifts**.
I understand that I am under no obligation to buy
anything, as explained on the back of this card.

225/326 HDL F42Z

Please Print

FIRST NAME

LAST NAME

ADDRESS

APT.#   CITY

STATE/PROV.   ZIP/POSTAL CODE

NO PURCHASE NECESSARY!

She instinctively moved in time with him. He didn't lead her into anything fancy, but he didn't just shuffle his feet, either. Other than holding her firm and close, he didn't make any other move to touch her. He didn't have to. She responded fluidly to every brush, every breath. And she didn't have to wonder if she was the only one feeling this, because the hardness of his body made it very clear he was along for the ride.

As one song blended into the next, Sloan pulled back enough to see her face illuminated in the soft glow of the torches. "Better now?" he asked.

"Of course," she said, hoping to brush aside any further references to the earlier upset.

"Those smooth moves made it look like you have experience defending yourself."

He'd never know how much. Instead, she shrugged. "Self-defense course at the Y."

He nodded but continued to watch her. At least she thought he did. Looking down, his face hovered over her in shadow, leaving her guessing. It should have been a relief to not see that intense purpose in his eyes, but instead the mysterious darkness both drew and scared her.

She knew just the way to redirect her thoughts.

"I'm starting to see what you mean. You talk a good game about company direction and expanding on buyers' demands, but...thank you for showing me."

His mouth opened as if he would speak, but then he brushed a soft kiss against her temple. "You're welcome."

As the song shifted into something a little rowdier, Sloan guided her off the dance floor to a secluded corner of the patio. The dry air was noticeably cooler, bringing gooseflesh to the surface of her skin. But the incredible view of the moon riding low in the sky over distant mountains distracted her.

"Ziara," Sloan said, his voice low and intimate. "I realize Vivian doesn't trust me—" The hand he raised to stop her words compelled her to pause. "I understand why she doesn't. Considering our history, she shouldn't. But I do actually know what I'm doing. Maybe the design part is new to me, but I've been buying companies and rebuilding them, sometimes after devastating setbacks, for more years than I care to count. I *can* do this."

His focus shifted out into the night. He leaned forward, resting his elbows on the stone balustrade. "But more than that, my father meant a lot to me. She thinks she's cornered the market on those emotions, but she hasn't."

Ziara recognized the ache in his voice from that first encounter in his father's office. "This really does mean a lot to you, doesn't it?" she asked, her voice barely above a whisper.

His head dipped as if in defeat, though she couldn't imagine him being defeated by anything—even Vivian's determined animosity.

"My childhood was wonderful until my mother died."

Ziara couldn't imagine how different her life would have been without her mother, how much better. "How old were you?"

"Fourteen."

She winced. "That's a bad age for major upheaval."

"Yes," he said with a slow nod as he looked out at the desert sky. "Her death was quick, only six weeks after she was diagnosed with a brain tumor." His pause was heavy with memories. "I had a new stepmother within a year."

What had his father been thinking? "It must have been hard for him to be alone."

"He wasn't alone. He had me." His deep sigh blew away any sounds of self-pity. "My father changed after he married Vivian," he said, the words slow but gaining speed. "Life became all about his new wife—her demands, her needs, her desires. What little was left went to his company, not to a fifteen-year-old boy in need of reassurance after losing his mother to cancer."

The picture of isolation he painted was nearly as bad as her own teenage years, living in her mother's house but not really *living* with her mother.

"She told my father I was lazy, unmotivated. But instead of wondering why, he simply condemned me. Any protests were considered a teenager's way of trying to weasel out of the consequences."

"And things never got better, even after you became an adult?"

"Not with Vivian poisoning his brain. At least, not that I could tell." He turned to her, the movement bringing them almost as close as they'd been on the dance floor. "He died from a heart attack, you know. Very unexpected."

Ziara had known, but he seemed to need to talk so she let him.

"When the lawyer read his will, I could hear Vivian screaming in frustration even though she never uttered a sound. The fact that he left me any part of Eternity Designs completely shocked her."

As if he needed some connection with Ziara, his hands reached out to rub up and down her arms, warming her from the outside in. "But that forty percent meant more to me than all the money, houses and stuff Vivian inherited. I could have sold it, resented it. But it made me think that in some small way, he had truly seen what I'd made of my life and was telling me that he believed in me."

An alien urge to wrap her arms around his waist and snuggle close swept through her. She just barely kept herself from acting. "Then why did you stay away so long?" If the company had meant so much to him, why had he left Vivian to it?

Laughter rumbled in his chest, the vibration echoing in her own and setting off all kinds of sparks under her skin. "You've seen how well Vivian works with me. For Eternity's own well-being, I stepped back from the running of it. She wanted free rein. I gave it to her."

"But you knew the time would come…"

"I knew without strong business acumen, Vivian probably couldn't keep the firm afloat. So I waited, and showed up when she didn't have a choice but to let me step in."

His cold calculation should disturb her, but what choice had he been given?

"Vivian should have known I wouldn't walk away forever," Sloan said. "Eternity is the only part of my father that I have left."

Which said all she needed to hear.

Eleven

Retracing their steps back through the house, Sloan found Patrick in the front room surrounded by people laughing. He gestured, letting his friend know he needed a moment.

Patrick approached with a casual, lanky stride. If he'd been into computers, he'd have been a geek, but he'd been designing clothes and dressing those around him for most of his life. He and Sloan had bonded as young men over the neglect of their home lives. Despite their many differences, Patrick was always the person to shake Sloan out of his anger, force him to look in a new direction or simply bust his chops until he could solve his problems. Sloan offered the same support, and they took every opportunity to dog each other about relationships, jobs and various life issues, just like the brothers they should have been.

Now Sloan needed something more than camaraderie. His thoughts must have shown, because Patrick flashed a rueful grin. "Do-or-die time, huh?" he said.

Sloan didn't disappoint. "Yep."

With a gesture Patrick directed them to his office. As Ziara moved into the space, she gasped. Sloan watched with a warm feeling in his chest as an almost childlike excitement burst over her face. He certainly understood.

The room was completely out of character with the rest of the house except for the pale walls and arches over the double windows. Otherwise, overflowing bookshelves lined every other wall, with more shelves jutting out to create aisles and hidden nooks. There were several oversize leather chairs with huge ottomans and a table-style desk supported by intertwined pieces of wood that formed the legs. It was slick, modern, but washed with an antique feel. An incredible contrast that Ziara obviously loved.

"This is so unique," she breathed.

"Patrick would live in here if everyone would leave him alone," Sloan said, earning a sucker punch in his upper arm.

"Would not."

"Would, too, you little recluse."

Ziara looked back at them in surprise, then glanced at the door separating them from the party.

"That's right, Ziara. Sloan calls me a recluse, but look at the parties I put on. He's clearly delusional. As is perfectly evident by his insistence that I join him in this crazy designing venture."

"I'm not giving up, Patrick. You have to give me an honest chance at talking you into this."

His friend waved toward the closed door, and the lavish house and glittering guests beyond it. "Why would I want to leave all this?"

"You know you get bored easily. This is just an opportunity for a new challenge." He might as well start off simple.

"You think working with fifty cast members and a demanding director isn't challenging?"

"How about—to teach an old nemesis she doesn't know what's best?"

Sloan noticed Ziara stiffen out of the corner of his eyes. Though her back was turned politely to them as she perused a nearby bookshelf, he still couldn't dismiss the connection he had to her every emotion.

His jaw tightened as he remembered seeing her fight off that drunk. Granted, the guy wouldn't get too far in a crowded party, but something about the practiced way Ziara had handled him made Sloan uneasy. What had happened to her that she needed to know how to defend herself? Classes at the Y, his ass!

He forced his attention back to Patrick. "Look, it's time to step up to the plate, buddy. We're leaving tomorrow. Are you following me or not?"

"I'd have to be crazy to sign on to pull together a show in less than three months."

Sloan grinned. "But think of the thrill."

"Vivian is not going to like this," Patrick said with a careful glance at Ziara. "The last time I did something she didn't like, she threatened to have me arrested."

Ziara gasped. "What did you do?" she asked.

Patrick had the grace to look away. "Well, we snuck into the liquor cabinet when she wasn't home and guzzled half the bottles down."

Ziara frowned.

"Give us a break," Sloan said. "We were only nineteen at the time. And how were we to know she had guests coming over for drinks the next day?"

Both men laughed, which felt good to Sloan. He missed those simpler times, when his struggles with Vivian only impacted himself and sometimes Patrick instead of the livelihood of close to a hundred people.

"It made an impression, that's for sure," Patrick said with a shudder. "Her expression…"

Sloan tried again. "So view this as the chance to show Vivian you've grown up from a spoiled little rich boy to an extremely talented designer."

"Flattery will get you everywhere," Patrick said. He rocked back on his heels, indicating to Sloan he was finally considering his offer without saying a word.

"I'm serious," Sloan said, stepping forward. "You don't need flattery. You know what you're capable of. You work on these live shows because it gives you something to do and an excuse to be here. Just give it a shot. If nothing else, just get me through this show."

This time Patrick leaned forward to meet him head-on. "I want final say on all designs."

Sloan shook his head. "Robert and Anthony would come unglued. They've been there forever. It wouldn't be right, Patrick. Besides, you would only be tweaking the main line with modern elements, not actually designing the clothes completely."

But Patrick wasn't swayed. "This isn't a power trip, Sloan. It's the only way I can have two lines finalized by fashion week." He glanced carefully around the room. "You do want the lingerie line ready for the show, too?"

Not looking at Ziara, Sloan inclined his head. He simply had to trust that this weekend had taught her all she needed to know. And that she'd stand by him—or at least near him—if Vivian went ballistic. "You would have complete control over that line. I want to open with both in two months."

Patrick stared at him for a long moment, then shook his head. "I can't believe I'm saying this, but yes—I'll do it. You are going to make it worth my while?"

"Always," Sloan agreed.

"Then I'll see you on Wednesday." Still muttering to himself, he left them to attend to his other guests.

Mission accomplished, Sloan's instincts set their sights on another prey, another conquest. As he and Ziara settled into the limo, his senses were attuned solely to her, the soft whisper of her breath, the smooth swish of her skirts as she crossed her legs, the spicy scent of her skin mixed with some illusive floral perfume.

His mind drifted back to this morning, watching her through the windows of the lingerie store. When she'd first entered, she stood almost paralyzed, looking so lost and unsure. So unlike herself. He'd almost dragged her back out rather than strip her of her usual strength.

But the point had been more important than protecting her. And now, he had the image of her explorations burned into his brain.

He was downright hooked.

Shame filled him as he remembered his casual thoughts about getting close to her in order to gain her loyalty. All it had taken was a true glimpse of her response and this game had become strictly personal.

Sloan slumped back in the seat, staring out the window of their limo. Getting Eternity Designs back on track was kicking his ass.

Ziara spoke into the darkness. "Well, you did it."

He couldn't tell from her tone whether she approved or not. Probably not. He wasn't worried. She was a walking example of what Patrick was capable of—the proof was in his design.

But Sloan didn't want to think about work. He'd rather have her in front of him so he could touch her, stroke her breasts until her nipples peaked—

"Yep," he finally got around to replying, his tone ironic but showing his fatigue.

"I hope Patrick knows what he's getting into. This time frame will mean a lot of late nights."

"He won't mind me working him like a dog," Sloan joked, chuckling when she looked askance at him. "Patrick may come from money, but he worked hard in school and at his job. He'll come through for us."

She nodded, but he still sensed her hesitation. There wasn't anything he could do about that. She'd see in time.

Her silhouette, profiled against the night, accelerated the beating of his heart. Sloan breathed deep, forcing calm to cover his growing need. He noted the slope and angles of Ziara's cheekbones. A model's face. Why did she work so hard to hide her beauty? He was more determined than ever to find out.

The conviction that she would be his surged deep in his soul.

He wanted to unravel the mystery, find what she hid beneath the surface so well. Why she hid at all.

"This is an interesting place," she said, her eyes focused on the approaching city lights.

He studied the thick dark lashes concealing her thoughts from him. "I'm glad you like it. Patrick takes a lot of pride in his work *and* play."

"It shows. But I didn't mean just tonight. More like Las Vegas in general." She absently rubbed the material of her dress between two fingers. "A combination of decadence, debauchery and the everyday. Kind of like life."

He scooted closer, gaining ground until he could touch her hair with the hand resting across the back of the seat. "How so?"

She dropped her head back so that it landed in his palm, but she didn't seem to notice. The silky weight of her hair made him want to run his hands through it, massage her scalp until she moaned, use handfuls of it to guide her mouth to all the places where he wanted to feel that wet warmth.

"Well," she went on, "maybe not everyone's life, but at least mine. My old life."

The opportunity opened before him like a lit doorway. Adrenaline aftershock, sleepiness and the shakedown of her natural barriers were lowering her inhibitions. The facade was melting away.

He told himself he should hold back, but they'd shot way past a professional relationship at this point. As he caressed her scalp, he knew deep down he would get to the bottom of the contradictions in her personality that had him tied in knots. For all the wrong reasons.

The intimacy of the limo, shrouded in gray shadows, invited him to explore the secret places, the dark desires beneath her surface. It would surely be the experience of his life.

"Rough childhood?" he asked.

Her eyes closed a moment as she shuddered. "You have no idea."

She turned toward him, those dark eyes sucking him away

from the voice of reason. "My mother…" She paused, biting her lip as if afraid to say more. "My mother was so wrapped up in her own needs, her little games, that she didn't care about what happened to me. She abandoned me."

Though he'd heard quite a few tales of childhood woe in his time, the desolation darkening Ziara's face ignited a protective streak in the pit of his stomach. "How old were you?"

Her fingers worried the fabric now. "Officially? Seventeen. Unofficially? So long before that I can't remember when."

Thoughts tumbled through his mind about what could happen to a seventeen-year-old girl who looked like Ziara without anyone to protect her.

"What about your dad?" he asked.

Her fingers jerked then went still. "I wouldn't know. I never met him." A few minutes passed before she said, "I think I could use a drink now."

Reaching out, he trailed his fingers down the back of her tense hand. "I don't think you need alcohol."

"Yes. I do."

"Why?" Sloan asked, taking the risk of looking straight into those tempting eyes. Half-mast lids were sleepy, sultry. Sexy. Man, if she decided to drink, who knew where they'd end up?

Her desire to let go had him shaking. It must be worse than he thought for her to resort to booze. "Why?" he repeated, hoping conversation would distract him from his thoughts and rapidly escalating erection.

"Because without it I'll never do this." She twisted, her lips brushing his, though she stopped short of a firm kiss.

The fire that burst through him burned away his inhibitions with one clean flare. "Ziara," he said, pulling her gaze to his. "You don't need liquid courage to do that."

Something perverse inside of him exulted in her making the first move, so he remained still. A quick lick of her lips sent a shiver of anticipation through him. Her lashes lowered as she pressed closer. Her lips barely met his before he took the reins back.

Burying both his hands in the soft fall of her hair, he stormed her mouth, sliding his tongue inside. Without further invitation, he explored the moist heat within before returning to caress her lips with his own. So soft, yet meeting him halfway, she beckoned and commanded his response without a word.

A flash of lights outside the windows eased Sloan from the cocoon of intimacy they shared. Though they were behind tinted windows and privacy glass, they were still in a public place.

And he wanted to do something they could be arrested for in public. Even in Las Vegas.

Resigning himself to a snail's pace, Sloan resumed his exploration of Ziara's mouth. He resisted the urgency surging under his skin. Their first time together shouldn't be in the back of a limo with a driver on the other side of the glass.

But he couldn't stop himself from exploring the boundaries a little. Drawing his hands down the side of her neck, he pulled her mouth closer, letting one hand travel to cup her breast. The soft weight overflowing his palm made him groan, but her electric response had him swearing.

Luckily at that moment they came to a stop in front of their hotel. Sloan opened the door himself and pulled Ziara out behind him. He rushed through the lobby and into the elevator with her a few steps behind. His hands trembled as he swept the key card through the lock, then pulled her into the suite with less finesse than demand.

The dim light of the suite was barely enough to silhouette Ziara's beautiful face. The stillness in the room as the door clicked shut only accentuated the pounding of the blood in his veins. He stalked forward, using their still-clasped hands to draw her near. He was pleased to see she didn't cower from him, from the intensity of his desire.

"Ziara, I need you."

This time it was she who anchored her hands in his hair. "And I need you," she choked out. "I really do."

Her voice shook at first but quickly firmed, though she sounded surprised. Whether at the need or the admission, he wasn't sure, but he didn't question his good fortune. Letting her pull his head down, he met her swollen lips once more, tasting the sweet burn he now associated with Ziara herself.

Allowing his hands free rein, they roamed her body, cupping those full breasts and squeezing them gently together. Her nipples hardened into peaks he could feel through the layers of fabric.

He followed the curve of her waist to the flare of her hips, finally drawing her tight against his erection.

Ziara bit lightly against his lower lip, sending Sloan's body and mind flying apart. Grabbing the zipper hidden along her side, he jerked it down, then the dress. Ziara gasped, but he didn't care. He just needed to touch her skin with his.

Instinct took over. His lips only left hers long enough to pull his shirt over his head. Drawing her against him, he groaned at the sensation of flesh against flesh, hotter than he could ever remember being. His head fell back, only to drop forward again to bury in her neck.

Her sweet, spicy scent drove him to taste her skin. Working his way down, he licked and nibbled the smooth column of her neck and the curve of her collarbone. He fell to his knees so he could savor the textures of her breasts and nipples.

Only then did he become aware of her panting breath, too jagged for passion. Releasing her sweet flesh, he looked up, catching the glint of moisture on her cheeks in the lights filtering through the far windows. "Ziara?"

"Please stop."

Twelve

Ziara stayed in her room the next morning until the last possible minute. Hiding wasn't the noblest of behaviors, but she simply couldn't face Sloan after calling a halt to...whatever last night had been.

How would she ever explain why she'd led him on, then left him hanging like that? How could she ever look herself in the eyes again and not remember her actions? Behavior that brought memories of her mother flooding to the surface. No matter how much her mind insisted she wasn't using Sloan, the fact that he was her boss couldn't be ignored. She refused to participate in anything reminiscent of her mother's life, built on sex, money and scheming for everything she could get.

Drawing in a deep breath, she smoothed her hair back into its usual bun. More aware than ever of the facade she presented in her business suit, she grabbed the handle of her rolling suitcase and opened the door. Sloan stood silent near the outer door, his own luggage not far away, remains of breakfast littering the table near the window.

Keeping her chin lifted and her eyes focused over his shoulder, she somehow crossed the room without stumbling or being sick. By the time she neared Sloan, his hand rested on the doorknob, but he made no move to leave. She could actually feel him looking at her, and her insides shivered. Part of her cowered in humiliation; the other part flared back to life with arousal.

For long moments Sloan didn't move, keeping them locked in a silent battle. The tension ate away at her composure.

"I just have one question," he finally said, his voice strained and husky. "Why?"

She spit out the words she'd rehearsed during the long, dragging hours of the night. "You're my boss. It just isn't right."

She must have managed the right level of conviction, because he opened the door and led the way outside. Watching him stride away struck her as bittersweet.

The flight home, long and silent, was punctuated by agonizingly polite phrases like "Excuse me" and "Would you like a drink?" Her body pulled in on itself, making her wish she could shrink into oblivion. But she couldn't. Not yet. Soon, though.

Unfortunately, Ziara was left with lots of time to think over what had occurred between them, as if she hadn't replayed it a hundred times in the dark of night. His kiss had been seductive in more than the obvious sense. It had made her blossom with beauty, power and wantonness. Therein lay the rub. She wanted to revel in the passion Sloan evoked, whether they were sparring or kissing. But she couldn't because it might lead to becoming the one thing she'd promised herself she never would.

As for work, she couldn't fathom how she'd ever behave normally again. Why did it have to be this particular man who affected her like this? The one man who could tear down the respectable career she'd worked so long and hard for with just a few words.

Deciding to bite the bullet as they stood at the luggage carousel, she turned and said, "Would you like me to pick up some lunch on my way to work?"

"Go home," he said.

Ziara's body froze with her emotions. She couldn't see for

a moment. Everything went blurry. When her vision cleared, Sloan was propping her suitcase in front of her. Was he so fed up, so desperate to be rid of her, he would fire her despite Vivian's insistence that they work together? Not that Vivian would oppose him once she found out what Ziara had done.

"Rest today," he said, his voice a little softer this time. His gaze inventoried her face, probably noting the swelling under her eyes and the red rims she'd been unable to cover this morning. "The real work starts tomorrow."

He turned and walked away without looking back, leaving confusion and an achy longing behind.

Desperately needing something to distract herself, Ziara tried to catch up on things she probably wouldn't have a chance to do in the weeks to come unless Sloan changed his mind about firing her before tomorrow. Deep cleaning the house and weeding the flower beds were always good for keeping her hands busy. Too bad her mind didn't want to cooperate.

But even if he didn't fire her, she knew in her heart she'd have to move on as soon as the show was over. Even if Vivian graciously extended the offer to be her executive assistant to Ziara, just knowing Sloan was right around the corner and could appear at any minute would keep her on edge.

It looked like she'd end up losing, after all. Her heart tightened, grieving as much for the loss of her beloved position within this company as it did for the necessity of keeping Sloan at arm's length. She hadn't just worked for Eternity Designs, she'd believed in its values, its purpose, and had hoped security could be found within its ranks.

As she went inside to clean up, she couldn't hold the tears back any longer. They mingled with the streaming water of the shower, invisible enough that she could dismiss her shame.

What was happening to her? All these emotions, so long buried deep inside, were erupting at every twist and turn. This was exactly why she didn't want them—because she couldn't control them. Or maybe she grieved because she did want them yet couldn't express them.

Guess she could add confusion to the messy pile.

Tears spent, she dried off, shaking away the last vestiges of depression and guilt. She dressed casually in khaki capris and a fuchsia T-shirt, then brushed out her hair in front of the bathroom vanity. Everyone was allowed one colossal mistake in their lifetime, right? This was hers. At least her conscience was clear. Her mistake wouldn't hurt anyone but herself.

Padding into the kitchen, she immersed herself in cooking dinner. Something as far from paella as she could get.

She threw together a quick southwestern chicken panini, which she coupled simply with apple and orange sections. Delicious as it was, she'd only managed to choke down half when the doorbell rang. Grateful for an excuse to give up on the pretense of eating, she straightened her T-shirt on the way to the door.

Shock sizzled through her when the door swung open to reveal Vivian. Without waiting for an invitation, her mentor glided inside. Ziara remained speechless for a moment. In the six years she'd been working for Eternity Designs, she'd never seen the Creightons outside the office. Now in the space of a week, both of them had shown up unannounced at her house.

After a thorough glance around the room, Vivian turned to face Ziara. "Is he here?"

Though Ziara understood, she still asked, "Who?"

"Sloan, of course."

Ziara easily pulled her facade into place, almost amazed at how well she could handle the accusation. But then again, she didn't have anything left to lose. "Sloan is not here, Vivian, and I resent the implication that he would be."

Vivian studied her for a moment, brows raised as if surprised Ziara would stand up for herself. Then her chin dipped in a slow nod of acknowledgment. Luckily Ziara found she could meet Vivian's eyes without a problem. A glimmer of compassion streaked through her as she noted Vivian's disarray, in contrast to her usually immaculate appearance.

"Perhaps we could sit and talk," Ziara said. She gestured Vivian into the sitting area facing the fireplace. The overstuffed chair and chaise weren't necessarily elegant, but they were comfortable and their deep burgundy hue complemented the fire-glazed tiles covering the hearth. "Can I get you something to drink? Coffee? Sweet tea?"

Vivian shook her head, a trembling sigh escaping her coppery brown lips. "That's what I so like about you, Ziara," she said. "Always cool under pressure, knowing just the right thing to say."

Ziara perched on the edge of the chaise opposite Vivian, wishing the same were true in her relationship with Sloan. *Business.* Business relationship with Sloan. They didn't have anything outside of that…anymore.

"I know my accusation was rude. But considering Sloan's history with assistants and this trip to Vegas…" She made a vague gesture with her hand, her diamond rings glittering in the soft evening light. "I assumed something I shouldn't have, knowing you. You are far too smart a girl to get mixed up with a smooth talker like my stepson."

Ziara prudently kept her mouth shut and her face impassive.

"Did Sloan procure a designer?"

Ziara now wished they'd go back to the sex issue. There were a lot less mines in that field.

Vivian grimaced. "Ziara, I'm going to find out eventually. I'd rather be informed now than surprised in front of my employees."

Ziara was too emotionally exhausted to come up with a clever sidestep. "He's hired Patrick Vinalay."

Vivian stood immediately, the *click* of her heels rapping on the wood floor. "I should have known Patrick would be the one to take him up on the offer. But it will put a kink in my plans."

Ziara frowned. "What do you mean?"

Vivian turned to face her, the pale cream of her skin contrasting with the bold colors of Ziara's home. "I thought I could get around whatever he might do by influencing Robert to cause a few delays until I could find a backer to bail me out, but having someone else on the design floor will change that."

With a jolt, Ziara realized how serious Vivian was about

this. Her mentor, the woman who had taught her the meaning of professionalism, had actually considered sabotaging her own company. Delays in production could have bogged down the rest of the process, resulting in major issues at showtime. Maybe even cancellation.

Unaware of Ziara's growing alarm, Vivian smiled and said, "I'll just have to find another way to get what I want."

Sloan paused for a moment after exiting the elevator, his pulse pounding as he stared at the door to his office suite down the hall. How ironic that after years of sidestepping persistently amorous employees, he now found himself on the other end, wondering how he could go back to acting like a normal boss. Especially when all he wanted was to lay Ziara across his desk and— He coughed to clear his throat. *This wasn't helping.*

If only he hadn't seen those red-rimmed eyes. Knowing how much he'd upset her, when she could usually be counted on as the calm one, put those boundaries firmly back into place. Determined not to cause any embarrassment, he marched forward.

"Good morning, Ziara," he said as he swept by her desk. "Could you get me the location contract, please?"

"Sure," she mumbled.

He took that for as good a sign as he was gonna get. They spent the morning focused on the push for the show, smoothing out location details and ordering fabrics Sloan already knew they needed.

Ziara left for lunch at 11:30 a.m. on the dot, but Sloan stayed behind, trying to breathe after a morning of straining to act normal and, honestly, trying to hide his erection. Once he had himself under control, he figured it might be a good idea if he headed down and gave the Old Brigade a heads-up. Patrick was due to be in sometime today, but he hadn't texted Sloan to let him know when.

Exiting on the third floor, he heard raised voices. *Oops. This visit was just a little too late.* He eased onto the overlook. Remaining back in the shadows, he studied the scene below. Patrick had arrived and no one was happy about it. Seeing

Ziara standing to one side of the fray, he made his way down the staircase and slipped up behind her.

Unable to resist, he leaned in close to her ear. "Did I miss the start of the war?"

In his chest, he felt the shivers that moved down her spine, urging him to press closer. How quickly his resolve was shaken by the temptation of almost touching that caramel skin.

His mind focused on the heat from the exposed curve of her neck and the vanilla scent drifting from the tamed confection of her hair.

"I ran into Patrick at the door," she murmured. "And made the mistake of letting him in."

Patrick was throwing out orders as if he owned the place, which didn't surprise Sloan in the least. Patrick knew how to captivate a room, but true resistance didn't bring out the best in him. No one appeared to be playing nicely.

"This is my studio and it will run the way I say," Robert bellowed.

Patrick folded his arms over his chest. "Really? When I signed on it was with the express understanding that final say would be mine."

Robert gasped, his hand clasping his heart, in contrast to Anthony, who stood silently in the background, watching the scene before him with somber eyes. "Say it isn't so!"

Patrick chuckled, prompting Robert to launch into a litany of French while Anthony's face turned red to the point of glowing. Sloan feared the way he bottled things up might cause a heart attack.

Taking control, Sloan let his voice boom out across the massive room, bringing everything to a halt. "That's enough."

Ziara jumped as he moved away from her, stepping forward from his position on the sidelines. "Patrick is here to modernize the line."

"But we don't need him," Robert insisted.

Sloan went on as if he hadn't spoken. "He will take the basic designs you put together and adjust or add to them as needed.

I have given him final say in the overall designs for the fall line to speed things up."

As Robert sputtered, Sloan pinned him with a look. "Do you want this studio to close?"

"No," Robert said, resignation in the very lines of his face.

"Then I suggest you find a way to make this work."

Not as diplomatic as he could have handled it, but effective. Sloan let his gaze sweep the whole group. "You two will put together the basic designs we've already approved, with Patrick adding what he believes is necessary. He'll have his hands full between that and his additional line."

"Additional line?" They all jumped as Vivian's voice erupted from behind them. "And what would that be?"

She walked toward the men, bypassing Ziara with barely a glance. Sloan's blood started to pound through his veins, that instinct to clash rising to the fore. But he checked himself, his curiosity starting to stir. How much had his little assistant given away already? He'd been with her most of the morning, but he couldn't account for every phone call, every second in the office. Or out of it.

"Still causing trouble, I see, Patrick," she said.

"Vivian." Patrick grinned. "As lovely and cold as ever."

She frowned but let the comment pass as her eyes swept over the men to rest on Sloan. "What do you mean, another line? We'll have a hard enough time coming up with one." She turned to examine Patrick from under raised brows. "Don't tell me he's going to do some kind of trashy, glitzy gowns. Surely taste hasn't gone that far downhill."

Why was she ignoring Ziara? He didn't want to believe that Ziara would rat him out, but Vivian was her mentor. Was Vivian testing him? Did she already know what was coming? The thought nibbled at the back of his brain. Ziara stood at the rear of the group, her brows lowered, arms crossed tightly over her stomach. Noting every curve, every shift, he still couldn't tell if she was transmitting nerves or guilt. He remembered her tortured expression as she'd asked him to stop—*please don't let it be guilt.* Deep inside, he needed her to be innocent, needed someone to be on his side.

"Actually, Vivian, it won't involve wedding dresses at all," Sloan said, going on the offensive.

Vivian stiffened. Enjoying himself, he let a smirk slip onto his lips. Even though Ziara's silent stare weighed heavy on him.

"Then what is it?" Vivian asked.

"He'll be launching our new lingerie line."

Sloan may have delivered the news with just a bit too much relish. The room became so still that from several feet away he heard Vivian's ragged intake of breath.

"Absolutely not!"

The furious look she threw Ziara definitively answered his questions—the woman he'd held in his arms, who clung so tightly to her professionalism that she would turn away from the inferno they created together, had stood her ground. Or rather, his ground. She'd kept his secret, despite the risk of losing the career Vivian held in the palm of her hand.

Now—if he didn't succeed, he wouldn't just lose the company. Ziara would lose everything she'd worked so hard to achieve.

Thirteen

Sloan and Patrick holed up in his office for most of the afternoon while Ziara practically collapsed at her desk. Work was beyond her for the first time in her life.

As if in slow motion, she relived Vivian turning until her accusing eyes met Ziara's. She knew Vivian would forever hold her responsible for not telling her about the lingerie line the day before. Her stomach clenched as the ramifications of her actions hit her. When Vivian turned and left without a word, Ziara had said her final goodbyes to the position she'd worked so hard to attain.

Vivian would never give it to someone she couldn't trust.

But would Sloan believe her now if Ziara came to him with the truth? She'd been trying all day to find the right time to tell him about Vivian's threat, but each time she'd hesitated. They'd maintained a strictly professional attitude toward each other that she'd been afraid to upset. That balance was so fragile. What would happen if she brought up such a personal subject?

"Wish me luck, sweet cheeks," Patrick said, sweeping by her toward the suite doors. "I'm off to face Mutt and Jeff."

She frowned, her strained emotions too heavy to hide. "Their names are Robert and Anthony."

He leaned against the doorframe. "It was just a joke."

"I know. But Robert and Anthony are going to have a difficult time adjusting to this. They've devoted many years to this company. Joking might not be the way to go."

A light grin tugged his lips. "I can take a hint. Just remember, I'm making the best of a situation they created."

Hoping her expression told him she understood, she nodded and watched him slip out the door. Then she dropped her head into her hands as the roller coaster of emotions of the past few days—heck, the past few hours—got the better of her.

She'd lost so much—her direction, her focus—and for what? Where would she go from here? Once Sloan got through the fall show she'd have to leave. But how could she find a job that would mean as much to her as this one?

"Ziara."

She heard Sloan's husky voice at the same moment that his heated palm cupped the back of her neck. She sensed him kneeling beside her chair, but she couldn't bring herself to raise her head, because she knew her face would be an open book at the moment.

"Ziara," he tried again. "Are you okay?"

No, she wanted to cry. Instead, she wiped the emotion from her face as she would tears, then sat up straight. She nodded shortly. "Yes. I'm just tired."

Skirting around her, he propped himself on the edge of her desk. She tried hard not to notice the sculpted muscles of her thigh, revealed by the pull of his slacks.

That husky drawl came again. "Do you need to go home?"

Like the snap of a twig, the pressure broke her prized control. She tilted her head to the side in order to face him. "Why are you being so nice to me?"

He choked on a laugh, those electric eyes widening. "Am I not supposed to be?"

"No. I mean, after..." She shook her head. "I'm not handling this very well."

"Me, either," he said, his voice deepening as he slid off the desk, then lifted her to stand before him. Using her arms to draw her against his chest, he bent to take her lips in a kiss that made no mistake as to his needs.

To Ziara's shame, she couldn't pull away, even knowing they were at the office. Her lips opened with a groan and her mind shut down. On a purely physical level, she met him pant for pant, kiss for kiss, lick for lick. Sloan's hands tightened to the point of pain on her arms, but it was one more sensation in the flood. Her control completely evaporating, she allowed him to lead her wherever he wanted to go.

Suddenly he pulled away, staring down at her, leaving her dazed and panting. "Not one word. Just go in my office."

Confused, Ziara thought he was speaking to her until she caught a glimpse of Patrick sweeping past. Her eyes snapped shut, her head dropping forward in shame. How could she have let this happen? Here of all places.

With a nudge of his fingers under her chin, Sloan raised her face. Opening her eyes, she noted his expression numbly at first, then with growing awe.

Instead of the crazed lust or judgment she'd expected, his eyes sparked with honest desire and a touch of tenderness. A reverence she'd never expected to receive from a man warmed the icy blue of his eyes. The look sent her own need into hyperdrive.

"I guess we'll have to put this discussion on hold," he said, tracing her moist lips with his thumb. His eyes narrowed in resolve. "But we will talk, Ziara, because neither of us is going to be able to ignore what's happening here."

Turning, he entered his office and shut the door behind him, leaving her to wilt into her chair. She should be worrying about Patrick—what he'd seen, what he assumed. She should be worrying about Vivian and her own future. Instead, she trembled inside, thinking only of Sloan's parting words.

Sloan and Patrick remained in conference so long that Ziara took the opportunity to slip out and head home. She desperately needed some time to herself, time to sort through her feelings.

As she concentrated on assembling lasagna for dinner, hoping the tedious layering would help her focus, she acknowledged that she'd had other reasons for calling a halt to things in Las Vegas. Reasons much deeper than Sloan being her boss.

Because, deep down, the thing she feared most was what might come the morning after. She didn't know how to do more, or whether he would want to do more...or if he would even care about the consequences. But every time he looked at her with that mixture of passion and admiration, she came a foot closer to crossing that inevitable line. She forced her mind to give it a rest as she focused on the task at hand. Sauce, noodles, sauce, ricotta cheese, mozzarella, then noodles again. Swaying slightly to the sultry jazz music playing through the house's sound system, she savored the feel of the cool tile beneath her bare feet. Breathing deep, she pulled in the smell of tomatoes and oregano enriching the air around her, blending with the darkness creeping down outside to cool the summer heat.

She'd just grated a small block of Parmesan onto the top and put the pan in the oven when the doorbell rang. An uncharacteristic expletive slipped out as she wiped her hands. The sound of her own doorbell now filled her with dread.

She barely got the lock turned when the door burst open. Sloan stalked through, slamming it shut behind him. Holding her gaze, he slipped the lock back into place, then strode across the small foyer to where she'd backed up against the love seat.

Without a word, his hands anchored in her hair, dragging her mouth to his. She had a brief moment to wonder about his obsession with her hair before surrendering to the dark current of desire.

Her body melted into his, her head automatically tilting to

the side to accommodate his mouth. When she made no protest, his hands slid from her hair over her shoulders and along her spine to cup her rear end, pulling her forward to meet his erection. With a groan, he pushed into the cradle of her hips. Her body arched, rising to meet his demands.

Before she could think, her shirt was unbuttoned. He peeled it open to reveal her breasts. Pulling back just the upper part of his body, Sloan spent moments memorizing the view. The pressure from below reassured her that he liked what he saw.

She wished she could see his hands as they cupped her through her bra, but she couldn't tear her gaze away from his face. Thoughts of losing his respect fled in the wake of the awe glowing in his expression, the utter pleasure he took in touching her.

Pride intensified her response. She wanted to revel in his reactions. Pushing herself farther into his hands, she shivered as a zing shot from her nipples to that all-important point between her thighs. The pressure there was heavenly yet growing more urgent with his every touch.

Allowing her head to fall back, she lost all strength as he sucked and licked his way along her neck. He anchored her to his body with his arm around her hips.

After pausing for a moment to savor the rapid pulse at the vulnerable base of her neck, he lifted her into his arms and carried her down the hallway. As if by instinct, he strode past several rooms with barely a glance, pausing outside only one.

"I should have known," he murmured, then strode across the room to lay her on the bed. Soft illumination from the doorway and a candle lit earlier glinted off the gold threads in the purple bedspread, the silky material caressing her bare skin when Sloan laid her down. After stripping her, he stood and tore off his own clothes, his gaze never leaving hers as he quickly slid on protection.

The sight of his body took her breath away. Long, lean muscles. Smooth, firm chest. Strong, tight thighs. Her core ached for the steely length between them. She wanted to touch him, savor every new discovery. But he was already crawling onto the bed and spreading her trembling thighs to his gaze.

The flash of vulnerability surprised her. She knew he wouldn't hurt her, wouldn't humiliate her. But the fears still lingered.

"Sloan, slow down," she gasped.

He stretched to take her mouth in a hard kiss before resting his forehead against hers. His panting breath sounded loud in the quiet. Only faint music could be heard from down the hall.

"I can't, Ziara," he said. "I've waited too long, wanted too hard. Please let me in now."

She hesitated, knowing that if she did, there would be no turning back. Already her hands and thighs shook with the effort of holding herself together, but her need was too great. She had to meet him all the way. As she'd feared, there would be no half measures.

And hopefully no regrets.

She groaned, her thighs sliding apart. Reaching down with a boldness that surprised her, she took him in her hand and guided him to her hot, wet entrance. He pushed inside with one plunge.

His body in hers sparked a tingly firestorm that burned between her thighs and spread outward to every point of her body. To the tips of her fingers, the top of her head. She could feel him imprinting on every part of her.

As he moved, the fire built higher and hotter. She'd never yearned to let go like this. Even though warnings screamed inside her brain, for once she thrust them away, so she could revel in how he made her feel.

She was drunk—not off wine, but off the sensation of having him so deep inside her, having him devour her with his gaze, having him stroke and praise her. His possession went straight to her head like tiny champagne bubbles.

With a cry, a sharp peak overcame her, but his whispered words in her ear brought her quickly to another.

The contractions were intense and powerful but not satisfying. As he levered onto his arms and pounded between her thighs, her body writhed, lifting to meet him, demanding more and more until she finally exploded in an outward expansion. Thousands of pieces flying out, a moment of nothingness, then floating back to make her whole again.

As she collapsed into the softness of the comforter, she heard Sloan shout. He buried himself hard within her body, holding stone still as he emptied himself.

A part of her, she dimly thought, then accepted him into her arms when he collapsed. Absently she stroked the slick muscles of his back, wanting only to keep this connection from fading so reality couldn't enter.

He groaned and moved against her but didn't try to leave. His mouth traveled up her neck, settling below her ear as he nuzzled close. Sensation stabbed into her nipples, and her hips lifted in response.

With an appreciative chuckle, he slowly pulled away, then disappeared into the bathroom with his pants after a quick brush of his lips over hers. Who knew when sex worked, really worked, that there were so many shocks along the way? With this man, only this one, sex had been one incredible sensation after another.

She lay in the bed, absorbing the quiet, but as she stared at the chiffon strips of material that formed her canopy, tension rapidly spilled back into her system.

What was she doing here? In the rush of sensations, thinking had been beyond her. As panic set in, she jerked to her feet, rushing through the room to grab clothes and drag them back on.

Her regular clothes didn't feel nearly secure enough, so she pulled a sweater from the closet and slid her arms inside, tightening its hold on her like a straitjacket. She stared into the dark depths of the closet, grateful for the nothingness for a moment.

Until her gaze focused in on her work clothes: suit jackets, A-line skirts, dress pants, severe button-down shirts. Work. She was a different person there. He was a different person— her boss.

The panic spread, making it hard to breathe. She didn't even hear Sloan until he was right behind her. "Ziara, are you okay?"

She didn't respond. She couldn't with her throat closing. When his arms reached around to circle her waist, she jumped, whirling toward him, then backing into the darkness of the closet in a misguided effort at hiding.

"Hey, it's all right," he said, his voice still as husky as when he'd been moaning in her bed. "What's the matter?"

Her head started to shake back and forth. "I can't do this. I really can't. We just can't do this."

She realized her eyes had closed, enfolding her in the darkness. After a deep breath, she opened them to focus on Sloan's face just inches from hers. His breath warmed her cheek.

"Talk to me, Ziara."

Sucking in air seemed a herculean task, but she managed, calling on years of maintaining a perfectly calm demeanor. When she could finally focus on Sloan in front of her, she took in his pale features without the protection of her normal walls. The thought almost started the panic again, but she shoved it away, tucking it down in a teeny tiny box to deal with later. Much later.

"I'm s-sorry…" she stuttered. "I've never had, whatever that was…"

"I think you had a panic attack," Sloan said. His shoulders dropped as he relaxed, though his hands continued to cup her face. "Are you okay?"

"I think so." *No, absolutely not.*

"Want to tell me what brought that on?"

"I…I…" Just one more deep breath. "I guess it just hit me. What happened. What—what we'd done."

He nodded as if her stream of consciousness made any sense at all. "Come here," he said.

When she started to follow him, she realized her muscles had turned into Twizzlers. She walked, but it took all her concentration to keep everything from wiggling all over the place. Wow. Since when did sex turn people completely unstable? Of course, she'd felt that way ever since she'd met Sloan, so this wasn't something new.

He led her to the overstuffed reading chair in the corner of the bedroom, where he settled and pulled her into his lap, all in one motion. Protest wasn't an option. He simply did what he wanted.

Unconsciously her fingers made short, light strokes across the top of his pecs, exploring the light smattering of hair that rested beneath them.

"I'm going to ask one more time," he said gently. "What's going on in that little worry factory in your head?"

Any other time, she would have smiled at the analogy, because it was pretty close to accurate. But right now she couldn't. "Sloan, this is completely wrong—"

"Doesn't feel that way," he said, his mouth nuzzling into the crook of her neck.

The shivers he elicited felt so good, but she gallantly reached for control. "Stop," she said, proud of her firm, no-nonsense tone, though her attempts to stand were promptly thwarted. "Sloan, you're my boss. I can't believe I lost my head long enough to forget that."

"I can." She didn't appreciate his grin. Her stern stare changed his tune. "Look. I understand this is a little unusual. But the fact is, I'm not technically your employer. Vivian is. And—" he continued a little louder when she would have argued "—I'm working with you temporarily. Once Abigail retires, you'll go back to working in Vivian's office."

Her frown drew tighter as she realized he hadn't come to the same conclusions she had. Vivian wasn't going to keep her on, no matter what. Better to change tactics. "You'll abandon the company?"

Luckily Sloan kept a hold on her when he jerked to his feet or she would have fallen. But he quickly let go to pace several feet away. He didn't give her a chance to get steady before he started speaking, his voice rough and low. "What the hell? Why would you think that?"

"I...I didn't mean..." Maybe it would be better to keep her

mouth shut. She truly wasn't sure where the question had come from, except she knew Vivian hadn't been worried about Sloan being around long-term. She chose the safe route. "I know you have other companies, other projects."

"Yes, but my father's company means a hell of a lot more to me than those."

Immediately guilt settled in Ziara's stomach. In her own panic, she'd forgotten the whole reason Sloan was even at Eternity Designs. "I'm sorry, Sloan."

For a moment he didn't move, his tall body a looming tower, his head lowered as if in grief. But when his head lifted once more, none of that emotion showed on his face. He crossed the short space between them to take her once more in his arms. "Look, this will be fine. I'm only your boss for a couple more months, at the most. Until then we'll keep this strictly out of the office."

She couldn't help but wonder if she accepted his reasoning simply to give herself permission to stay right where she was, burrowed deep in his warmth and masculine scent. But for once she was going to do what she wanted, not what the job required. "Agreed," she whispered.

After a thorough kiss, Sloan cocked his head to one side. His nostrils flared as he breathed deep.

"What's that smell?" he asked.

Sniffing, Ziara caught a whiff of Sloan's citrusy scent, followed quickly by the sharp tang of burning cheese.

"Oh, no," she said, rushing toward the hall. "The lasagna."

Fourteen

Ziara was able to salvage most of dinner because only the outer edges had burned. Sloan found this very amusing and teased her as they ate.

"You are a great cook," he finally said. "Who taught you?"

She picked up their plates and crossed to the sink, feeling a little too vulnerable still to face him. "I taught myself." Turning on the water, she rinsed the plates. "My mom…worked a lot. I had to either cook or live off cheese and crackers."

Not wanting to elaborate, she concentrated on cleaning up. Ever since her brain had come down from its mind-numbing high, she'd been struggling with conflicting emotions. She didn't want to enjoy being with Sloan, and the fact that she did—although *enjoy* was way too mild a word for how she was feeling—was something she might not be ready to face. Being with him intimately hadn't been dirty or sordid or even ordinary. And it wasn't just the sex she'd enjoyed, it was the eating and talking and laughing.…

Ziara was so lost in thought that she didn't notice Sloan approaching until his warmth cradled her back. "What are you doing?" he asked, his hands resting on her hips. His moist lips nuzzled through her hair to the back of her neck.

More than anything she wanted to melt into his warmth, to experience again the joy of being a part of him.

"I—I'm cleaning up. What does it look like?"

"What if I want some more?"

Twisting in his grip, she tried to see his face. "Why didn't you say something? You can have another plate."

He closed in, his hips tight against her backside, giving her an unmistakable impression of his hardness. "I didn't mean more food."

Her breathing accelerated, currents of excitement jumping from his hands straight between her thighs. She wanted to stroke back and forth, letting every inch of her back discover every inch of his front. Then she'd turn and repeat the moves all over.

He was an addiction. A tempting treat. She could discover every texture and taste of his body, branding him as hers with her scent and touch. As his hands traveled from her hips to her breasts, she wondered if she was losing her mind.

At least she was enjoying the ride.

He turned her to face him, claiming her mouth with his. Slowly unbuttoning and unzipping her capris, he allowed them to slide down to the floor around her feet, followed quickly by her panties.

With a flex of his biceps, he lifted her onto the tile counter. A squeal rang out as her bare bottom met the chilled surface. He chuckled.

"That's sadistic," she accused.

He grinned, his dark gold hair falling softly from the crown of his head to frame his devilish good looks, reminding her of a Hollywood bad boy.

"I'm all about the sensations," he said.

The grin quickly melted into a more serious look, making her feel like prey. Her heartbeat picked up again, and she tried to pull him to her, but he didn't budge. Layers disappeared:

her sweater and cotton T-shirt, followed by the tank she'd put on in lieu of a bra.

He kissed her thoroughly, letting his hands trail down her arms, which he guided behind her and propped on the counter.

When he released her mouth, she found herself leaning back on her braced arms, her body on display for him to peruse at his leisure. Instantly awkwardness swept in. How could she let him see every little part that she'd kept hidden for so long?

When she tried to lift herself up, his hands on her shoulders held her still. After one dark look, his gaze moved down... along with his hands. She should have felt shamed, wanton in this position, especially when he pushed between her legs and propped her feet on his hips. There was absolutely no-where to hide.

She let her head fall back and her eyes close. Therein lay her only protection from his onslaught.

Before he finally entered her, he had explored each and every part of her body with thorough intent, branding her with his touch.

She didn't recognize the moans and whimpers erupting from her mouth. She only knew if she didn't have him, she couldn't make it through the next few minutes. His body in hers was a momentary relief, but when he thrust deep, the fire returned ten times hotter. She exploded within minutes, Sloan following close behind.

With their ragged breathing echoing off the tile, she didn't even care about being put back together again.

Pulling himself out of Ziara's bed at two-thirty the next morning wasn't an easy or pleasant task for Sloan, but he forced himself to return to his own house. They needed to slow down—and certainly needed to downplay anything that smacked of a relationship, sexual or otherwise.

He'd tossed aside Ziara's concerns last night and he stood by his decision on both counts. But he knew no matter what he'd told her earlier, Vivian would kick her to the curb the minute she discovered they were sleeping together. She was only barely tolerating Ziara after learning about the lingerie line.

So he'd stay in control. They'd be careful. He could have her and protect her—somehow.

When he'd suspected a mystery lay beneath Ziara's cool exterior, he hadn't known the half of it. He felt like he'd cracked that hard surface and found the richest pool of tempting dark chocolate, so deep he could drown in her.

Willingly.

That was the scary part. Her loyalty, her integrity, her professionalism—all wrapped up in the sexiest package he'd ever touched. It made him want the very thing he was trying to hide: a chance just to be with her. He couldn't articulate the why of it. It was just Ziara.

Coming through the door to his office suite seven hours later, he barely controlled his double take. There sat Ziara, looking as calm, crisp and professional as she always did. He couldn't reconcile it with the woman who'd wrapped her silky, toned legs around his waist while he gave her multiple orgasms the night before.

Looking at her now, he wanted to kiss color into her lips and cheeks. Better yet, make her eyes glint with mischievous passion. But that was in direct violation of their agreement. He barely controlled the impulse to rip every last pin out of her hair until it fell in a black cascade down her back.

Wouldn't Vivian just love that?

As if sensing a presence, she glanced up from her desk, eyebrow raised in inquiry. A tentative smile peeked from her lips—not her normal professional greeting, but a small, secretive smile full of the knowledge of what they'd done to each other the night before.

He stalked to her desk and leaned forward onto his hands. "I want to tear your clothes off."

Her eyes widened a bit before returning to normal. Her lips pressed together as if to contain a laugh, though it didn't disguise their sensual fullness. "Shh, not in the office. Besides,

Abigail called to say Vivian wanted you on the design floor in twenty minutes. A reporter is coming to interview y'all."

He cursed under his breath. "Guess I'll have to put my plans on hold until tonight then. The least you can do is come along and protect me from the big, bad dragon lady."

He paused, giving her a moment to back out. Her subdued "Sure" swept through him like a victory dance. He wouldn't jeopardize her reputation here at work, but he had to have her again. Soon.

Fatigue hovered at the edges of Sloan's consciousness a few hours later. The reporter had been excited about something new and different to feature in an upcoming society page, and had snapped at least a hundred pictures of the design floor.

Ziara had tried a few times to head back up to the office, but Sloan or Patrick always distracted her before she could get away. Constantly conferring with her over details of the actual show and even some of the fabric choices had kept her in close range—exactly where Sloan wanted her.

But she'd definitely started to lag at the end, her normally calm tone growing short and her posture tight. The most trying thing, the one thing that seemed to tap her energy while revving up Sloan's, had been Vivian's disapproving stare. Oh, she'd managed to keep it out of range of the camera, but Sloan could feel the bad vibes emanating from her on more than one occasion. At least she seemed to be an equal opportunity dispenser of disapproval. No one but the reporter and Robert could do any right this morning.

Sloan just wanted to crawl back under the covers and sleep, right up against his naked assistant. Problem was, lunchtime had barely arrived.

"Check out the feature in the Sunday paper on the seventeenth," the reporter threw back over her shoulder as she and the cameraman swept from the room.

Sloan could see his own weariness reflected back at him in Patrick. "Is it just me," his friend asked, "or was that woman way too perky for anytime before lunch?"

A giggle slipped from Ziara's lips, but she quickly went silent under Vivian's disapproving gaze.

"Considering how quickly we're trying to pull this together, we should be grateful for all the publicity we can get," the stern matron said.

Ziara backed slowly away, disquiet leaking through the cracks of her professional facade. Patrick simply raised a brow and turned away, letting the comment slide over him like water off a raincoat.

"Ziara," Sloan said, ready to get away from the old witch himself. "Let's head back upstairs and get some work done before the whole day is gone."

They arrived at the elevators together, slipping in just as the door opened, not realizing Vivian had joined them until they turned back to face the closing door. *Damn it. Would this day never end?*

"Since I realize a written report is a bit too much to expect from you, Sloan, why don't you bring me up-to-date on where we stand at the moment?" she said.

Not seeing the point of haggling, Sloan gave her a quick rundown of the current budget and status on the design work. By the time he finished, they were in the upper hallway and Ziara was eyeing the door leading toward their office—and away from Vivian—with desperate yearning. Sloan couldn't blame her. Vivian's shoulders tightened the longer Sloan spoke, even though he presented the facts in a clear, dry manner. Any minute now she was gonna blow her top.

"And when are you planning to show me the designs for the…lingerie?" Vivian asked, making the word sound like trash to be picked up from the side of the road. *Ah, here it came.* "Or were you planning on surprising me, just as you did with Patrick?"

"I didn't realize you expected me to run every idea by you, especially since your approval isn't necessary," Sloan replied.

Ziara pressed her lips together, her tension palpable. This did have all the makings of a pissing match and for once he'd rather be anywhere else. Like in Ziara's cozy, colorful bedroom.

"I simply think that running things by me would show a little decency, since I am still the majority owner of this establishment."

Sloan kept it short, but not sweet. "Decency isn't part of our agreement."

"You mean not a part of your agreement—or hers, I'm learning."

"That's enough, Vivian."

She chose to ignore Sloan's warning, turning the full force of her ire on Ziara. "You were supposed to be keeping an eye out on him, keeping me informed."

"I did," Ziara said with quiet dignity, though Sloan read unease in her carefully guarded expression.

"About everything?"

"Ziara is doing what she thinks is right for this company," Sloan interrupted. "She loves Eternity Designs and wants to see it regain its rightful place in the market, just as I do."

Vivian shot another glare over Sloan's shoulder, so palpable it probably burned Ziara's skin. "What's best for Eternity isn't her decision to make. It's mine."

"Typical of you, Vivian. Last I remember, your decisions ran this place into the ground." Sloan's voice was laced with so much venom he was surprised any of them were left standing. Years of resentment and loneliness surged inside him, anger over losing his father breaking through the surface. "Drop it. Ziara's doing a damn good job bringing this show to life. She can't do that and be at your beck and call all the time. Or don't you remember how much work that really is?"

If anything, Vivian's gaze turned positively glacial. "What I remember is all the work I've put into keeping this company afloat. Your father's dream has kept me going since his death."

"And you've shut me out," Sloan fought back. He was in rare form today. "But that's what you wanted, wasn't it?"

"I did what I thought was best, what *your father* would have wanted."

Sloan stalked closer, the carpeting muffling his steps. "If

Father wanted me out, why would he have bothered leaving me forty percent?"

"How would it have looked if he'd left his son with nothing?"

"You know, Vivian," he said, "I don't think he cared about how things looked nearly as much as you do."

The truth hit really hard, and Vivian's face flushed a mottled red. "I will not let you ruin me."

"If I wanted to, you couldn't stop me."

Sloan turned and walked away, calling Ziara to follow him. But the memory of Vivian's face remained with him for the rest of the afternoon.

Outrage? Yes. Anger? Yes. But something else, something underneath that hinted at desperation. What would Vivian do if she felt that Sloan had backed her into a corner? If he succeeded, would Vivian rejoice in Eternity Designs's success or ruin it for the chance to keep her position as its CEO?

And did his lover have any idea what might be coming their way?

Fifteen

A few days later, Ziara stalked down the hall after a frustrating hour mediating between the two-ton egos on the design floor downstairs. As if her emotions weren't shaky enough! She could barely restrain herself from yelling, *Behave like the adults you are or I'll send you to time-out like you deserve.*

But she'd managed to keep her prized cool. Just barely.

Since their confrontation with Vivian, the cracks in her professional facade started by Sloan's lovemaking had widened. Vivian's rejection hurt, more than the taunts of her childhood, but she'd pushed through to do whatever she could to make this show a success. She owed Eternity Designs and Vivian that much, even if Vivian didn't want it.

Deep inside she'd convinced herself that Vivian would change her mind once Eternity Designs regained stable footing. She'd understand Ziara's decisions, instead of condemning her—and somehow Ziara would be able to remain a part of this home away from home.

Somehow.

Finally reaching her desk, she sank into the seat and swiveled to face the desktop. Exhaustion lowered over her like a heavy mantle. The long days of tension and emotional turmoil—good and bad—were taking their toll. As she dropped her head into her hands, her elbow connected with something on her desk. Glancing down, she found a long, rectangular present wrapped in iridescent paper. Her mind remained blank for long moments, but slowly trickles of excitement filtered in.

Gifts were few and far between in her life. The small Christmas presents exchanged in the office and with a couple of neighbors were the extent of her experience. She almost couldn't believe someone had gotten her something special, something just for her.

Lifting the box, she found a piece of Sloan's personal stationary underneath: "Enjoy, Sloan." With delicate care, she peeled back the paper, revealing a flat, black jeweler's box with feminine gold lettering: Par Excellence, Las Vegas.

Old fears made her drop the box like she'd discovered a big, hairy tarantula was living inside it. The simple package filled her with dread despite her commonsense knowledge that it was just a box, a small gift of appreciation. Giving herself a firm talking-to, she reached out to pick it up with a fairly steady hand.

Her heart started freezing before she even had the lid open. By the time the teardrop diamond pendant, hung on a delicate gold chain, came into view, she'd gone completely numb.

"Is that from your trip to Vegas?"

The unexpected sound of Vivian's voice made Ziara jump. She almost never came to Sloan's office, preferring to send Abigail when she needed something. What sin had Ziara committed to condemn her to Vivian's presence at just this moment? The layer of distaste underlying Vivian's tone compounded her own churning emotions.

"I suppose so," Ziara said, too shaken to play defense. With a deep breath, she looked up at her former mentor.

Vivian watched her for a moment, her gaze then moving to the sparkling necklace. "You are a dedicated employee with the tact and control to excel as an executive assistant, Ziara.

I've been extremely concerned by your behavior since you took this position."

"I don't understand," Ziara said, her words more forceful than she would normally have used with her employer. She shook her head. "I thought you trusted my judgment? You are the one who put me here."

Vivian nodded. "That's because I thought you had the ability to fulfill the position where others had failed. Without becoming personally involved. Now I know I was wrong."

"I thought you wanted me to insure Eternity's success—that's what I'm trying to do."

"By worming your way into Sloan's bed?"

The words stole Ziara's breath, cutting through the cold, but Vivian wasn't through with her.

"Oh, I know how this works. I was even accused of it myself. No one understood what my husband and I had, how we felt about each other." She raked her eyes over Ziara's trembling body, encased in a perfect pink suit, with harsh judgment. "But I never stooped to using my body to get what I wanted."

If she could have doubled over in pain, Ziara would have. Instead, she felt locked in a swirling fog that mixed old accusations with new ones. Vivian turned toward the door but paused before leaving. "Ziara," she said without turning around. "Rest assured, if Sloan doesn't get rid of you when he's done, then I will. There's no place at Eternity Designs for smut like you."

Her exit was as quiet as her arrival.

With an unnatural calm, Ziara put the lid back on the box. The memories called up by the piece of jewelry had more power to hurt her than even the threat of losing her position here. Under normal circumstances, she could have buried them quickly and gone about her day, but these weren't normal circumstances.

Rising to her feet, she walked into Sloan's office without her usual knock. He looked up in surprise from the papers he'd been perusing on the desktop. "Was that Vivian I heard out there?" he asked.

He glanced from her face to the box in her hand. "I saw that in Vegas. I hope you like it."

Leaning forward, she placed the box squarely on his desk in a parody of the way she'd found it. He looked up in confusion, allowing her to meet his gaze straight on.

"Just so you know," she said, her voice calm but hollow, "I don't require payment for services rendered."

Then she turned on her heel and stalked out.

As dusk deepened to full dark several hours later, Ziara heard Sloan's Mercedes purr into her driveway. She'd been half expecting it, half dreading it. The stubbornness of his personality wouldn't let him leave her alone after their earlier scene.

And she wasn't anywhere near ready for him to be here.

Her eyes were probably still puffy from crying on the way home. She hadn't cried in a long time, but twice in a month was unheard-of. The emotional release after everything that had happened proved inescapable.

The loss of control bothered her because it wasn't *her*. She was the cool one, stable, clearheaded. But today she'd turned into a crying, hurting mess, desperate to close the door on a past that had reared its ugly head despite her attempts to get as far away as possible.

And it was All. His. Fault.

Not waiting for him to knock, she jerked the door open as he marched up the stone walkway. Pressure built inside as her anger swelled. Anger at him. At Vivian and her accusations. At the gift. At her lack of control. At her need for him, even after everything.

Catching sight of her in the doorway, he stopped short in surprise. "What do you want?" Because if he thought he was getting sex, he was sadly mistaken. No matter that her body clamored at the sight of him. The latent desire added another layer of dirt to her already soiled soul.

"Can I come in?"

Those commonplace, even words destroyed the last of her manners. Turning away, she left the door open for him to enter if he wanted to—she had no doubt that he would, even though she made it clear he wasn't welcome.

She stopped moving in the middle of the living room. Turning to face him, her arms instinctively crossed over her stomach to protect herself from any ugliness to come. She thought she'd escaped all the drama when she'd finally moved from her mother's house. But like her shadow, it had a way of catching up with her.

Sloan carefully—too carefully—closed the door, then approached her with cautious steps.

"Do you want to tell me what's going on?" He paused, and when she didn't answer, he continued. "Or am I going to have to drag it out of you?"

The anger that crept through her like lava spurred her to speak. It strengthened her backbone and lifted her chin. "I thought I made myself clear at the office."

"You think I'm paying you for sex?" His incredulous tone jarred her.

"I'm your employee. We...slept together. Then you gave me expensive jewelry. What am I supposed to think?"

That full mouth twisted. "Oh, maybe that it's a *gift?*"

"Vivian certainly didn't think that."

His eyes widened when he heard his stepmother's name. Ziara squeezed her arms tighter, hoping to hold in the tide of hurt and anger. She should have known going for a guy outside the safe zone would leave her feeling like a slut. So her self-image was a little skewed—years of bullying at home and school would do that. But Vivian's words had convinced her that she was repeating history.

Everything she'd felt for Sloan up until now—the dizzying rush of desire, need and freedom—wasn't pure at all. Just shameful. No one really needed another person that strongly. It had to be a mirage, a fantasy.

"What does Vivian have to do with this?" He stepped closer, one measured movement at a time. Ziara retreated until the back of her knees hit the side of the chaise.

"She came in while I was opening the box."

"Convenient, seeing as how she rarely comes to my office."

She glanced away. The logistics didn't matter now. Just the broken pieces left behind.

He reached out to tilt her face up, giving her no choice but to look at him. "She accused you of sleeping with me." His mouth tightened, compressing his lips and whitening the edges. "I don't care what Vivian said. She has no proof," he continued when she neither confirmed nor denied it. "Her view is a little skewed, black-and-white in a world of gray. She sees me as some kind of playboy, when the opposite is actually true."

Ziara couldn't stop her eyebrows from lifting.

Sloan chuckled. "Yes, I know it's hard to believe, but I've actually had to let three assistants go because they pursued me, not the other way around. This—" he gestured between the two of them "—is new to me, believe it or not."

He slid onto the chaise, pulling her back until her shoulders met his solid chest. "This isn't about me taking advantage of you because you are an employee, you're convenient or even because you're so damn hot. I thought…"

She leaned into his warmth, her spine too weak to keep her upright. Even though she knew it was wrong, her chest ached with her need to believe him. "So what is it about?"

"I don't know," he said, reaching around to cup her cheek in the warmth of his hand. "But I sure want to find out."

His kiss was gentle with a touch of erotic edge. She melted into him, afraid to believe, yet afraid not to. Old fears were hard to kill off. Like horror movie villains, they seemed to rise constantly from the dead.

Finally he pulled back. Standing, he picked her up, then re-settled them both onto the chaise with her firmly planted on his lap. "I saw the necklace in Las Vegas," he said, his hands already burrowing into her hair to excavate the pins confining it. "I don't know why I bought it. I just knew it would look stunning nestled right here." He brushed his knuckle across the hollow at the base of her throat. "Bright against your skin."

She shifted, swallowing hard. "Then why give it to me today? We agreed to keep this out of the office."

He laughed softly, a kind of exasperated sound that rumbled against her chest. "I honestly didn't think about it. I thought it might be a nice gesture after all the hard work you've done, and, well, Vivian hasn't been easy on you. I wanted to do something nice for you."

He felt so good, so solid beneath her hands. Looking up, she let her eyes meet his, the bright blue mesmerizing in the near darkness. Would it hurt anyone but her if she believed him, just for a little while? She'd lost everything else during this debacle. Why should she have to give him up this soon? Surrendering with a sigh, she melted into the crook of his shoulder. "I'm sorry."

He shrugged. "What made you think I intended it as a pay-off?"

She knew she shouldn't say it. But the words snuck out of their own volition—without her consent.

"There was an…incident when I was younger."

"What happened?"

She shouldn't tell, she couldn't. No one in the intervening ten years had ever known.

As if he were listening to her thoughts, he pressed a soft kiss to her temple and murmured, "I'll trade you. Tell me something about you, and I'll swap it for something about me."

The temptation, coupled with the darkening shadows in the room, coaxed the rest of the story from her.

"When I was a teenager, one of my mother's many…boyfriends…showed up at the house one day while she wasn't home. He said he was there to see me, to give me a present."

She snuggled closer, seeking Sloan's protection. "He gave me a beautiful ruby necklace. It was gorgeous, but even at that age I knew something wasn't right about him giving it to me." Her stomach clenched in remembered dread.

"Just then my mother came home. When she saw the necklace in my hand, she had a fit."

The accusations had been the worst—much worse than getting slapped and having the "gift" snatched from her hand. Her mother had accused her of trying to steal her client, not listening to a word Ziara said in her own defense. "Finally, he convinced her it didn't mean anything, but I stayed out of his way from then on. The way he watched me…"

Sloan's body absorbed her shudder. It felt so good not to be by herself anymore. She'd been alone, entirely alone, since that day so long ago.

Despite his promises to her mother, that man had tried to come into her bedroom one night. But she'd managed to slip out the window before he'd finished picking the simple lock.

Under cover of night, she'd watched him walk around her bedroom, touching her things. The next day she'd made a trip to a local hardware store, where a nice old man had sold her everything she'd needed to install a dead bolt. Ziara relied on herself alone after that. Until the day of her seventeenth birthday, when she'd left home without a forwarding address.

Ziara looked up at Sloan. Those memories from long ago influenced her current decisions more than she'd like to admit. "I shouldn't have jumped to conclusions."

"Just remember, not everyone thinks like Vivian does. Just look at Patrick. He's always telling me how great you are." He smiled, though his eyes didn't warm in color, and carried her to bed. "It's been a long week. Let's get some rest."

Gently, he stripped them both. Leaning over, he settled them against the pillows in a move that seemed natural to him. Ziara remained stiff for long moments before gradually relaxing into his hold. Never had she lain in another person's embrace, not even the loving hold of a parent. Until Sloan. Here with him, like this, felt like home. Warm, secure, safe… The final bit of awkwardness melted away.

"Tell me something now," she said, eager to shift the focus. "Tell me about your father."

She'd never had one, couldn't even imagine what it would be like to have a man in the house. Her mother's men had just been visitors who had brought nothing but indifference at best, anger and pain at worst.

Sloan's hands rubbed up and down her arms, lulling her into a drowsy state. "My father was always laughing, always happy, until my mother died. They were very much in love through it all." His hand started to squeeze, massaging up and around her shoulder. "I'll never forget, one time when she was really bad off with the cancer, he took me with him on a business trip."

"Where did you go?"

"I don't even remember, but I know we went to some kind of trade show. I remember following him through walls of people, listening to his voice as he talked to other men, having him introduce me like I was one of the adults, soaking it all in as he explained stuff to me."

His heartbeat thudded evenly under her cheek. "Did you learn a lot?"

"I was thirteen years old. I still remember every word."

As she drifted to sleep, the happy wistfulness in his voice brought on dreams of a family she'd never had.

Sixteen

The fast-approaching deadline for the fall show escalated the rush to complete the two lines, so the days got busy and the nights even busier.

She ran messages back and forth between Sloan and the design team and mediated a few squabbles, though the three designers had formed an uneasy truce among them. Vivian lay low as the time for the fall show approached. Ziara occasionally wondered how she felt, but no longer had an in to inquire how Vivian was doing.

She and Sloan spent most nights together, always at her place, with Sloan never staying all night. She didn't protest. What was the point of trying to force him into something he didn't want?

Only one night did they deviate from the pattern.

Sloan and Patrick had been holed up in a conference until about forty minutes past normal shutdown time. Ziara knew she could leave, but her greedy feminine nature urged her to wait. She could ask Sloan if he wanted her to cook dinner. If he'd like to unwind with a drink, a hot shower, a... She groaned, allowing her head to fall forward into her hands. Shameless. She was utterly shameless.

"Night, sweet cheeks."

She jerked upright, returning Patrick's smile as he sauntered out the door. Blushing, she turned to find Sloan leaning against the doorframe connecting their offices.

"You look tired," he said, his gaze scanning her face. "Am I driving you too hard?"

His sensual tone added deeper meaning to his words. She shook her head, her throat too tight to speak.

He reached for her arms, rubbing his hands along them in light, comforting strokes. "Why don't you go ahead home?" He nodded toward his open office door. "I still have some work that needs to be finished tonight."

She knew she should do exactly that. She should go home, rest and have a good night's sleep. Nibbling on her lower lip, she realized she didn't want to do what she *should*. That wasn't how she wanted to spend her evening. Studying the fatigue darkening Sloan's normally vibrant eyes, she realized she wanted to take care of him. Ease a little of the strain he was under. She chose not to wonder why but to just act.

"Why don't I go get something for dinner and bring it back here?"

As surprise lightened his eyes, she spoke faster. "It would save you some time. You wouldn't have to stop working as long and could get done sooner. I don't mind—"

The rush of words ended when he placed his lips over hers. She leaned into the gentle kiss for a moment. He pulled back until their lips barely brushed against each other.

"That sounds great," he breathed.

Her chest flooded with warmth as he pressed his mouth over hers once more, then returned to his office.

She tried not to be overly pleased as she raced home and changed into a gypsy skirt and tunic that she belted low on her hips. Though she never went out anywhere without her hair confined in some way, tonight she let it down and brushed it, the long strokes heightening her anticipation.

Sloan's obsession with her hair only grew. He was constantly touching it, burying his hands in it, especially as he rode her to climax. She was anxious to see how he reacted to her wearing it down at the office, even if it was after hours.

She stopped by a replica fifties diner near the office and ordered the deluxe burger and fries Sloan indulged in every so often, with a chicken salad sandwich for herself, before rushing back. When she walked through the office door, his eyes scanned her slowly from the tips of her strappy heels to the crown of her jet-colored hair. His gaze narrowed as it returned to her face.

"Oh, you so don't play fair," he said.

Her laughter floated around them as they spread the food on the small table in Sloan's sitting area. They ate in silence, staring out the floor-to-ceiling windows at the city lights. His eyes frequently rested on her hair. It felt so good to be free, to enjoy the moment.

"Why do you and Vivian fight so much?" Ziara asked, her earlier concern about the older woman still lingering in her mind. "It isn't just the business, either. You two seem at odds about most everything."

Sloan took his time chewing and swallowing. Ziara thought he wouldn't answer, though his face remained relaxed and open.

"She married my father when I was a teenager. I'm sure that rough adjustment period set some bad patterns in how we relate to each other."

He took another bite, chewing slowly, distracted by his thoughts. Her eyes strayed to the working muscles of his jaw and throat.

"My dad and I had a pretty laid-back arrangement until she came along. I don't know if she told him to take me in hand or what, but after their marriage it was rules, rules, rules and 'this is how we expect you to act.'"

"At the risk of sounding clichéd, at least someone cared," she said, forcing any self-pity from her voice.

Besides the dead bolt she'd installed on her door, she'd

stayed as far from home as possible. Often she ended up being at the public library until closing. She'd gotten a job at the local drugstore at sixteen, working her way up to assistant manager, saving every penny until she could leave town and lose herself in Atlanta. Her mother hadn't cared about her while she was home. She probably cared even less now.

His eyes snapped in her direction. "Do you know how Patrick and I met?"

"You said you met in high school."

He nodded shortly. "And he was my roommate in college. I was assigned to that room because I listed my original major as fashion design."

Ziara frowned. "I didn't realize—"

He broke in. "Vivian hated the idea. She told my father that I'd need a business degree if I wanted to run the company one day. He decided if I didn't change my major, he'd cut me off."

And he still hadn't gotten to run the company. The urge to defend his younger self rose, but she choked it back. "You and Patrick remained friends?"

"I know Vivian thought it was to spite her—and we got a kick out of rubbing her nose in it." He grinned. "But Patrick and I had become close by then. He taught me a lot about the design business that my father never did."

Just as Ziara was learning a lot more with Sloan than Vivian had ever taught her. "And he was the first person you turned to when you needed…a designer," she said, standing up to gather their trash.

"And he expects nothing more of me than to be myself and work hard to create success. I respect that."

As he came up behind her and kissed her on the neck, she wondered if he'd added the last bit for her benefit. Was he telling her what he needed out of a relationship?

No expectations? No commitment?

She frowned. She wouldn't be one of those women who turned into a clinging vine the minute a man showed any interest. As she shifted in Sloan's arms, she vowed to do the same as Patrick. She would enjoy the part of Sloan she had for as long as she had him.

She savored his hold until his guiding touch turned her toward him.

"I've waited long enough," he said.

He pulled her over next to him on the leather couch. She had a quick thought that she must have truly lost perspective to be doing this in his office before she could only focus on Sloan and his hands in her hair.

Later, much later, she woke alone on the couch. Disoriented, she sat up. Cool air caressing her skin reminded her of her nakedness. She grabbed the blanket Sloan must have covered her with and wrapped it over her shoulders.

Glancing around, she spotted Sloan hunched over his father's drafting table near the window, absorbed in the paper before him. He didn't look up as she hastily dressed, noting the clock read nearly one in the morning.

Walking to where Sloan stood, she peeked around his shoulder. To her surprise, the drawing was one of the designs for the fall show. The lingerie designs.

The table was covered with drawings in various stages of completion. They were classically beautiful—delicate, colorful and feminine—not slutty as she'd feared from the first. The designs were delicately sexy, with an exotic flavor that drew her.

"These are beautiful, Sloan," she said.

He grunted, seeming lost in thought. "What they need to be is finished."

She smiled. If she knew anyone who thrived under the pressure, it was Sloan. He might dislike—okay, hate—external expectations, but when it came to his expectations of himself, he didn't just meet them. He exceeded them.

But she was surprised by these drawings. They were his. Sloan's. Not Patrick's. Not Robert's. Not Anthony's. Sloan drew with sure strokes, bringing the design to life by catching the fluidity of the fabric, the lace detail and the fit against the body beneath. Compared to the one design sketch he'd shown her before, these were easily Picassos. And he'd kept them secret from her all this time.

She felt blown away—a bit sad that he hadn't told her before now—but blown away, nonetheless.

The scratch of pencil on paper continued a moment; then he froze. With extra care his eyes lifted to meet hers.

"Hey there," she said, residual emotions sharpening her tone just a bit. "Remember me?"

His jaw worked, allowing her to gauge the tension gripping him. Keeping her voice calm and free of accusation, she asked, "Were you ever going to tell me?"

"I don't know."

Um, ouch.

Something of her reaction must have caught his eye because he started throwing out excuses. And they actually made sense. "I've always drawn, always wanted to learn more about design, but never got the chance once I changed my major. After Dad died and Vivian forced me out of the company, I didn't see the point. But I've always wanted to try."

"Is Patrick some kind of front?"

His smile was a bit lopsided. "Hell, no. He's had to give me a crash course ever since he came home. Without him this would be a disaster. I've drawn up building plans for years." He looked over the pages before him, a kind of fascinated pride brightening his already light eyes.

"But why keep it a secret?" She struggled to keep disappointment out of her voice.

His mouth twisted. "You've seen how Vivian reacted to Patrick. Do you think she'd have signed any kind of agreement if she even remotely knew I would be in on the actual designs? Hell, my ideas for the show were shot to hell and back, but in the end she had no choice but to accept it." His naked shoulders lifted in a shrug, drawing her attention away from his sardonic grin for a moment. "It was one less battle to fight."

Which made sense, but she couldn't help wondering why he

hadn't told her. Didn't he think she'd understand after everything they'd said to each other, done with each other?

Maybe he didn't trust her as much as she'd thought he did.

Returning to the scared-rabbit mentality of her childhood had never been one of Ziara's life goals, but these days she found herself fearing the world around her like that lost, lonely child once more.

She wasn't entirely sure how to stop it. Throughout the next week, anxiety rolled over her whenever Sloan wasn't with her. Even though it was a stupid, feminine insecurity, she realized she wasn't as immune to the disease as she would have hoped.

Which was why she was awake at seven o'clock on a Sunday morning instead of curled up in the arms of the only man to ever inspire her to snuggle. He'd slipped into her bed after a really late night at the office and slept the morning away. But here she was trudging to the kitchen for some coffee, rather than waking him up.

When a knock sounded on her door, her heart jumped. *Please don't let that be Vivian.* All she needed was to confirm Vivian's already glaring accusations by having Sloan walk out from her bedroom in his favorite pajamas—his birthday suit.

When she opened the door, she stood for a moment in puzzlement. The woman's face wasn't familiar to her, but one look at her clothes and Ziara almost had a heart attack.

"Mom?" she croaked.

Her mother cracked her gum in the same way she'd been doing all her life. "I told you not to call me that, remember?"

I've done my best to forget. "Sorry. What can I do for you, Vera?"

"Aren't you going to let me in?" she asked.

Ziara didn't move, but shock kept her from shutting the door in her mother's face. She'd never prepared for this scenario, never dreamed her mother would track her here to Atlanta—or even care enough to want to find out where she was. This situation was completely alien, but anger started to seep around the edges of her confusion.

She wasn't about to taint her home with even a hint of bad memories. Pushing forward, she met her mother on the porch and closed the door firmly behind her. "What are you doing here?"

Vera knew Ziara better than to play the loving-mother card. "Well, I saw your picture in the newspaper, looking all fancy, prim and proper. Almost didn't recognize you."

Probably because she hadn't seen Ziara, truly seen her, since before she'd hit puberty. "That doesn't explain what you're doing here, at my house."

"Well, if you wanted to hide, you shouldn't put Z. Divan in the phone book. I picked up on that right off."

As her mother prowled the porch, Ziara performed her own inspection. The years hadn't been kind, by any means. Not surprising, since her mother had started binge drinking about a year before Ziara left for good. Her once-thick, shiny hair had been teased to lift its lifelessness. Wrinkles radiated from her mouth as if she'd taken up smoking, hard. But one thing remained the same: her clothes. The skintight animal prints hadn't looked good ten years ago, much less now.

"Right nice place you've got here, Ziara." She paused to peek inside the window along the side of the door. "Right nice. I always knew you would land on your feet."

I certainly did, with no help from you.

As Vera droned on about the house, Ziara found it easy to shut her out. There were no excuses, no changes her mother could make to establish a relationship between them—if that's what she was looking for here. Seventeen years had been opportunity enough. Even if it made her a bad person, she wasn't going to soften her heart for a woman who would put men and money ahead of her own child.

A child who had been haunted by those choices for her entire lifetime.

"Yep, you've done good. Better than I expected."

"I know." Anger seeped into Ziara's voice, making it hard and cold.

Vera stopped in her tracks as if just now getting the message. Her eyes homed in on Ziara, almost closing from all the mascara gooped on her lashes. "Guess you did get some of my genes, after all."

"Excuse me?"

Reaching into her cleavage, Vera pulled out a crumpled piece of newspaper to wave in front of her. With a quick snatch, Ziara was staring at the picture. In the foreground stood Vivian and Robert, discussing something with the reporter, but it was the background that caught her attention.

She and Sloan faced each other across one of the fabric tables. She looked as circumspect as she always did at work, but it was his expression that gave away the true nature of their relationship. She could just imagine the wolfish comment that would accompany that look on his face. Someone would have to be searching to notice, but she was pretty sure Vivian would look closely if given the chance.

Vera turned back toward the window. "That boss of yours looked like he could eat you up. Judging on his looks and money, I'd let him if I were you."

A shudder worked its way down Ziara's spine, the picture of Sloan even now sleeping in her bed burning in her mind. Despite the differences in their incomes, Vera and Vivian probably viewed this situation in a very similar manner. But what she felt for Sloan couldn't be reduced to a simple paycheck.

"Why are you really here, Vera?"

The other woman's back stiffened. "Well, I figure I fed and clothed you for seventeen years. Now that you're on your feet, payback would be the grateful thing to do. I've had a few setbacks lately, and I can't work—"

I just bet you can't. "Actually, Mother, the state paid for my raising. I took the checks to the bank every month, remember? I bought the groceries with the food stamps I managed to salvage from your purse. *I* raised me. Not you."

Anger sparked in the other woman's faded brown eyes. "I don't think so, you ungrateful brat. I worked on my back every day, something you never appreciated. And now you're going to make sure I never have to worry about money again."

Ziara crossed her arms over her chest. "This is ridiculous. Why would I give you money?"

"Because you want your next job to last longer than this one."

She froze. "What is that supposed to mean?"

"I could pay your boss a little visit. Put a little bee in his ear. After all, you certainly didn't earn those skills on your own. And I can do the same to your next boss, and your next, and your next. I'll follow you around like a bad penny until I get what I want."

Even though it was something she'd feared her entire adult life, she found herself saying, "They won't all hold me responsible for your actions."

"No, but they can hold you responsible for yours. After all, you did sleep with your boss, didn't you, dearie?"

And wasn't that the pickle she'd put herself in? Vera couldn't prove anything, but Sloan would know the truth. She had slept with him. Could she make him understand it was for love…not for money? Feeling sick, imagining what this woman would say to Sloan, she sank against the brick wall. "What do you want?" she mumbled.

"A salary of my own. You'll pay me every month to keep my mouth shut and stay at home. A nice home, not that nasty trailer I'm living in now."

Anger returned with the strength of a lightning bolt. "Like hell I will." She stalked closer, now the hunter rather than the hunted. "I'm not going to pay you a dime, *Vera*. I've paid enough for being your child. I'll just go to the police—you know blackmail is a federal crime, don't you?" Ziara wasn't sure whether it was or not, but her mother wouldn't know the difference.

Vera paled, backing toward the door. "You can't do that."

"Oh, I can and I will. Who do you think they'll believe, Mother? Me or you?" Securing Vera's arm with a firm grasp, Ziara led her off the porch and around to the driveway. A beat-up Chevy Cavalier rested at the curb, looking barely capable of going twenty miles, much less the eighty-five between Macon and Atlanta.

"Just remember this." Ziara turned Vera to look at her. Staring into those brown, sad eyes, Ziara felt her heart softening but forced steel into her voice. "I will not be manipulated. Neither will Sloan. So get back in your car and drive south. I don't want or need a mother anymore. I never did."

She waited until Vera pulled away before returning to the house. Once inside with the door firmly locked, she rested her head against the solid wood. She wouldn't cry—Vera had lost that hold on her a long time ago. She wouldn't worry—surely her mother wouldn't risk prosecution in order to get money from her. She wouldn't relent—Vera had made her bed a long time ago.

It would just be nice if she didn't have to stand her ground all alone.

Then a warm heat covered her back as Sloan brushed her hair aside to rain quick kisses across the base of her neck. "Good morning, gorgeous," he whispered against her skin. Her entire body came alive under his touch. "Did I hear you talking?" Ziara's heart started to pound, a dragging *thud, thud* that physically hurt in her chest. No matter how much bravery she could manage to Vera's face, telling Sloan the truth wasn't what she wanted. If he never knew her dirty, rank secrets, he would never look at her with pity or indifference or judgment. Even she wasn't that brave.

"A neighbor," she mumbled. "Just a neighbor who dropped by. Want some coffee?"

He growled, teeth scraping her skin this time. "I want something—but the coffee can wait until later."

Seventeen

"I think I'll head back to the office until you finish throwing your little temper tantrum."

Sloan winced as Ziara's words rang throughout the design floor, then turned to watch her dramatic exit, her body moving with the grace of a runway model and the irritation of a woman putting up with a difficult man. He'd snapped yet another order at her, one time too many, and apparently she'd had enough. He knew he took on bearish qualities the closer he got to a deadline. It hadn't bothered him before now.

But it wasn't simply the pressure that had him up in arms.

Ziara had been distant since their night here at the office. As he turned to Patrick to discuss the finer points of an orange flame pajama set, he remembered again the pure rightness of having her sleep in his arms before tearing himself away. A sense of inevitability colored every intimate moment they spent together. He couldn't decide if he was sinking fast or had already drowned—which only upped his grizzly bear aura of the moment.

Hell, there wasn't time to examine his life. He had a show to put on. Looking up, he found Patrick watching him. "What?" he demanded, not bothering to mitigate his irritable tone with his closest friend.

Patrick's face cleared. "Showing her the designs, huh? I thought you weren't big on anyone seeing them until they were done?"

Sloan shrugged, wishing Ziara hadn't let that little tidbit slip. "She was working late with me." He cringed at once again sounding like an uncaring ass, but he didn't have to explain himself.

"Does Vivian know?" Patrick asked, though his tone said he already knew the answer.

"Hell, no. I don't have to report my love life to her."

"Not about you, maybe," Patrick said, his tone unconvinced. "But she'd be interested in Ziara. You're poaching on her territory, professionally speaking. And she could make Ziara's life mighty uncomfortable after you leave."

"She already has, though Ziara admitted nothing."

"Please tell me you aren't going to leave her to face the old dragon alone when all this is over?"

"Who says I'm going anywhere?" he asked, then walked away without waiting for an answer. He knew he'd woven a complicated web. And he knew staying away from Ziara wasn't an option.

There would be plenty of time to fix all that *after* the show. Ziara's job was important to her, but he could always find her another one if he needed to keep them together. But he worried, deep down, that the approaching show was the reason behind Ziara's slowly rising wall. Was she afraid he would dump her after she was done being useful?

Deciding a quick exit was best for everyone involved, Sloan headed straight for the door instead of back upstairs to his office. He could get things done just as well from home and he wasn't in the mood to deal with interruptions. A brisk walk to his car would help with the thoughts crowding his brain.

The voice calling his name didn't register at first as the list of everything he needed to handle this afternoon ran through his mind. When he finally heard it, he turned back but didn't see anyone he recognized on the lightly populated sidewalk. A woman detached herself from the background to approach, but she wasn't familiar.

Her shaky smile revealed yellowed teeth from cigarette smoking if the bitter smell was any indication. Her clothes would have been indecent on a woman thirty years her junior, but on her... He kept his gaze trained on her face to spare them both any embarrassment.

"Are you *the* Sloan Creighton?"

Great. Media coverage could benefit a project, but it could also bring out the crazies. "Yes. How may I help you?"

The preening seemed instinctive for her, but it had Sloan shifting in his suede shoes. He glanced around—was he being pranked?

"My name is Vera, Vera Divan. I wanted to talk to you about my daughter."

Daughter? Surely not— "You mean—"

"Ziara? That's the one! She's turned into a right pretty thang, hasn't she?"

A part of him frowned in disbelief, though he made sure it didn't spread to his face. Judging by how she measured up against him, she was probably a couple of inches shorter than Ziara and the distinctly exotic flair was definitely missing. Maybe Ziara's father had been Indian, because it certainly hadn't come from her mother, whose thin, mousy-brown hair lacked her daughter's vibrant color. But a glance at her clothes revealed that they'd seen better days, sparking a moment of sympathy.

"Did you want to see Ziara, Mrs. Divan?"

"Oh, it's *Miss*. I'm not married, never have been—and I'm definitely available."

Sloan had been in many uncomfortable situations over the years, but this was one he doubted he'd forget.

"No, I didn't come to see Ziara. I came to see you after I found this." Reaching into a flashy, bright pink tote bag, she pulled out a newspaper clipping. Yet another article about their interview, but not from a newspaper that he recognized. He examined the photo. The look on his face as he talked to Ziara had him choking. They stood in the background, but the camera had still captured what was obviously a very intimate exchange.

"I'm pretty sure you get why I'd want to have a little chat, right?"

That caught his attention real quick. Though he had a feeling he wasn't dealing with a lady, he acted the part of the gentleman. With a sweep of his hand, he gestured for her to join him. "Would you care to walk with me? I'm heading to the parking garage."

Her grin was way too happy for his taste. Sloan wasn't fooled. Better to get down to business if this was headed where he thought. "What can I do for you, Miss Divan?" he asked, stumbling over the name.

One of her overly arched brows lifted even higher at his directness. "Well," she hedged, "I was just surprised as all get-out to see that picture in our local paper." She glanced sideways as they walked. "I'm from Macon, you know."

He didn't. Ziara rarely talked about her past, her family. The few tidbits he'd gleaned while in Vegas and since then hadn't painted a pretty picture, so he didn't push for more. He certainly couldn't imagine this creature giving birth to Ziara's exquisite perfection.

"But I know men," she was saying, "and a man only looks at a woman that way when he wants one thing."

Sloan jerked to a stop, swiveling to face her with tightly leashed aggression. "What the hell are you saying?"

"Not that I blame you," she said, her tone sweetly placating. "Ziara grew up around that kind of stuff. I'm glad to see she learned how to take care of herself and get what she needs. Guess she was paying attention after all. Too bad she has trouble with the follow-through."

Sloan's stomach went into a nosedive, swirling on the roller coaster before he could get off the ride. Please, please let her not be saying what he thought she was saying. He took another thorough look—short skirt, top unbuttoned enough to reveal more than the edges of her bra and abnormally high heels. In that instant, something in his memory clicked, and he recalled the woman he'd seen walking down Ziara's driveway last Sunday.

Ziara had said she'd been speaking with a neighbor. And he'd believed her. After all, he'd only seen the woman from the back—a quick glimpse out the bedroom window.

"Are you saying—"

One short, manicured finger scraped from one of his shirt buttons to the next, making his skin crawl. "That's right, honey. I'm good. Ziara learned from the best, all right. And now she wants you to pay up."

Anger started to build, low and deep. He'd spent the past five years since his father's death determined to take back from Vivian what he thought she'd stolen from him—the only piece of his father he had left. But Ziara proved even more ruthless than him.

Her mother was a prostitute. Had she truly followed in her footsteps?

There was no mistaking the insinuation. The woman before him lived the lifestyle, whether she simply used men for their money or actually walked a street corner. Ziara went in the opposite direction, had buttoned down every part of her personality. That would be why she'd latched onto Vivian, the exact opposite of the woman who'd raised her. Dressing to fit the part so she could catch even bigger fish.

The enormity of what she had done hit Sloan in the gut like a physical blow. He just prayed he didn't spew all over her mother's imitation designer shoes.

"Why isn't she here, asking for whatever the hell it is you want, herself?"

"Well, she's still a little soft when it comes to closing the deal. Not quite enough experience. When she asked me for help, I knew I'd have to step in. You'll do just as I ask." She waved the picture under his narrowed gaze. "This picture tells me most of what I need to know. Not to mention the words from Ziara's own mouth. That little trip to Las Vegas got things off to a right start, didn't they? I wonder how your stepmother would respond to accusations of sexual, um, what's that called?"

"Sexual harassment," he mumbled.

Though he knew she was wrong, and had defended his actions in the comfort of his own mind, there wasn't a whole lot he could say in his defense if charges were brought against him. And Ziara knew it.

"What, exactly, are you trying to exploit from me here?" he asked.

"Now, you don't have to say it like that." She glanced around the cool darkness inside the parking garage. "It's more like, you scratch her back, then well, you scratch my back. You've already gotten your scratch, I'm sure."

Her rough laughter had the bile rising in the back of his throat again. How could Ziara have viewed their time together as a business deal? As a bargaining chip? "Why not just come to me if she needed money?"

"Oh, money isn't what we want. Yet."

He waited, welcome numbness starting to creep through his limbs. For the first time in his life, he couldn't summon his hardball negotiator side.

"This little show you're working on? You're gonna walk away before it's done."

If the first demand hadn't shut him down, this one would have immobilized him. "Why would you want that?"

"Ziara knows it means a lot to you, but having Miss Vivian in charge means a whole lot more. Ziara owes her for all she's done, and with Miss Vivian as a boss, she'll have an executive assistant job locked down for years to come. Better deal than working for you until you get tired of her."

With each word, his disbelief was chipped away into nothing. Only one person could have told her those personal details—Ziara herself. As much as he didn't want to believe, it looked like he didn't have much choice.

"What difference does it make to you?" he asked.

"Well, it means a lot to me." She rubbed her fingers together in an age-old expression of greed. "With Ziara's status, I'll get myself a whole new makeover and access to an upscale client list." Her yellow-toothed grin said she believed this delusion. There wasn't enough plastic surgery and cosmetic dentistry in the world.... "Then we'll both be living large." She sidled a little closer, forcing him to back up flush with his car. "A woman my age could use a little retirement fund, so to speak. Of course, if I had someone like you in my life, I wouldn't need one, would I?"

"And if I refuse?" There was always a catch.

"Well, you wouldn't want Ziara's secrets to get out, now would you? With your reputation, how many people wouldn't believe claims of you takin' advantage of the hired help? Those big-money contracts wouldn't come your way nearly as often, if people around here didn't want to be associated with you, huh?"

He wasn't going to show how unnerved that made him. If Atlanta was suddenly filled with accusations of sexual harassment at his father's company, no one would risk hiring him. Ziara and Eternity would look like the victims, thus keeping their reputations solidly intact while his crumbled.

One of her nails tapped the newspaper clipping. "So what do you say?"

He struggled to find a way out of this mess, but his brain remained stuck on the picture of Ziara, sleeping so innocently on the couch in his office. Disbelief still hung around because he did care, didn't he? He'd fought it, hid from it, pretended it wasn't there.

But it was.

Knowing she had him backed against a wall, he conceded. "Done."

Ziara took a deep breath of cool air, savoring the softening fall weather, before pushing through the revolving door into the Eternity Designs building early on a Thursday morning. She felt much lighter after a good night's sleep, although she'd missed Sloan's warm body curved around her as she drifted off. Amazing how quickly she'd gotten used to that.

Now she was ready to face the Abominable Snowman again.

A soft laugh escaped as she crossed to the elevator. Sloan's attitude had finally pushed her over her limit, but when she'd smarted off in return, she'd felt a surge of adrenaline. Matching wits with him energized her, made her feel alive like she hadn't in her entire life.

She smiled as she trekked down the hallway toward Sloan's office, remembering a similar walk several months ago. Now, instead of dreading seeing him, she couldn't wait. Instead of resenting her attraction to him, she reveled in it.

Turning a corner, she spied Patrick standing in the doorway to her office. He gestured for her to hurry.

"Ziara, get in here."

Ziara rolled her eyes. Patrick tended toward the melodramatic, but she accelerated in anticipation of seeing Sloan. Even when he acted like a bear, he was a lovable bear.

At the thought, her body froze, her heart seeming to stop, then start again twice as fast. She could almost feel the shell encasing her heart give one last crack before bursting into a million tiny pieces. Left behind was a pure red, bigger, more feeling muscle that beat with the certain knowledge of her feelings for Sloan.

How did she even know what she felt? It wasn't that she'd ever been in love before. Or loved anyone at all that she could remember. Maybe her mother at some point, but she retained few memories from her early childhood. She remembered very little before her tenth birthday. After that Ziara supposed she'd lost hope of it ever being returned, so whatever love she might have had died a painful death.

The only love she'd ever felt had been for her job.

Maybe that's how she knew this was love—she'd never felt like this before, about anyone. She'd never felt so exposed, so vulnerable. So alive.

Patrick practically vibrated with irritation. "Come. On."

Ziara jumped, then picked up speed as she moved toward him. "What?" she hissed.

Patrick started dragging her across the office before she could even finish the word. "You have to stop him—"

Her heels skidded as she halted just inside Sloan's office. He stood in what she thought of as his "thinking" position: facing the floor-to-ceiling windows, head down as he contemplated those scurrying below him, his shoulders broad and square, hands clasped loosely behind his back. The surveyor of his domain.

After a moment, she took in various boxes littered around the room, file drawers gaping, the top of his desk wiped clean.

Her head swiveled from one end of the room to the other, not comprehending the chaos before her.

"He's leaving."

Ziara turned to find Vivian, the jolt of shock racing through her brain down into her body. "What?" She heard her voice but never felt her lips move.

"He's leaving." Vivian's tiny smile smacked of smug superiority. "Even though this means he'll lose everything, he's decided 'everything' is no longer worth his time."

"That's not what I said at all, Vivian," Sloan growled, though he didn't turn from the window.

Vivian practically purred in her victory. "But it's what you meant, isn't it, dear?"

"I told you, I have another project that needs urgent attention. There's only so much of me to go around." His voice sounded tight, no hint of emotion seeping through.

What? Ziara's brain could barely process what was happening. Another project? What about his father's legacy? His connection?

Her gaze fell on the drafting table in the corner where she'd watched Sloan, his golden head bent forward in the lamplight, hair long enough to obscure his face. Those drawings weren't the work of someone who didn't care, someone who could simply walk away.

Pivoting slowly, she faced Sloan, who stood just as he had when she came into the room, completely oblivious to anything happening around her.

At first he didn't move, but his back straightened, becoming more rigid. Something she hadn't dreamed possible. His hands tightened around each other. Could he feel the weight of her stare between his shoulder blades?

She waited for some sign that the man she loved at least gave a damn about something, about the people involved here. Unlike Vivian. "Was it all just some kind of game?" Ziara asked. "Didn't it mean anything to you?"

He twisted, marching down on her like a bull, forcing her to retreat. "You don't get to ask questions, got it?"

He turned to Vivian, facing her with a mixture of anger and despair like nothing Ziara had ever seen. "You got what you wanted, Vivian. Now get out. If I see you again, I might just change my mind."

Vivian's voice rumbled in the background, but Ziara couldn't make out the actual words. It didn't matter. Only Sloan mattered. The sound of the office door shutting with harsh finality shook her composure.

She was left in the room with someone she didn't know, didn't recognize underneath the stone cold facade. Oh, she should recognize him, remembering Sloan's first confrontation with Vivian. But that harsh strength had never been used against her.

Never.

With the numbness slowly creeping over every part of her body, she remained frozen as he approached once more.

"I hope this is all worth it for you, Ziara."

She shook her head. "What?"

"All the lies and deception. Why would you pretend to be something you're not? Why would you present yourself as this—" his hand gestured down her body, encased in a conservative black suit "—professional, moral woman, when deep down, that's not who you really are at all?"

Ziara felt her head start to spin. The words coming from his mouth had an eerie similarity to thoughts that had whirled through her brain for ten years. She'd told herself that she was a better person, a stronger person, than the trash heap she'd crawled out of— But sometimes it seemed she hadn't shaken it at all.

How had he learned her secret?

Her voice a little shaky, she said, "I don't know what you're talking about, Sloan."

Reaching out, he pulled a thick strand of hair from her loose updo, twisting it around his fingers like he had hundreds of times before today. Only this time, his touch had an edge to it, a slight pull on the roots that communicated his anger. "Really? Are you sure, Ziara? Didn't you know this would get to me a lot quicker than dressing like a tramp?" he asked, stepping close enough for her to feel his breath across her forehead. Those icy blue eyes gave no mercy, showed no love. In light of her own recent revelation, his lack of emotion hurt all the more.

Why was he doing this?

"I met someone yesterday," he murmured, the usually seductive tone now hard as a rock. "I met your mother, Ziara. Are you sure you have nothing to tell me?"

She almost choked, but forced out, "My mother?"

"Oh, I understand why you wouldn't volunteer the information. After all, this is a rockin' body you've got going on. Wouldn't want me to get a clue too soon."

He thought she'd used him for—what? Sex? Hadn't all those late nights and intimate conversations, all the hard work she'd put into building her reputation and work ethic, meant anything? "It is not what you think."

"Oh, she spelled it out pretty plain for me...unless you have a different explanation?"

"My mother is—" In that moment, under his hard stare, years of shame and fear kept her from saying the word *prostitute*. His obvious disgust told her he'd already come to his own conclusions. Knowing her mother, she'd given him every reason to believe Ziara had followed in her footsteps. And living in a small town had taught her that most people enjoyed believing the worst about others. She'd hoped he'd see her differently than other men.

But he hadn't.

"Sloan, please understand—"

"Oh, I understand. I understand that you used me to get what you wanted."

What?

"Or should I say what you and Vivian wanted? I guess I can live with the fact that no matter what happens, I'm the one who actually lifted this place back onto its feet." He turned back to the drafting table, running a hand along its edge. "The only person whose recognition I've ever wanted is long gone. So why should I bother seeing this through? After all, I've gotten everything I wanted from you. And plenty of it."

"Sloan," she moaned. How could this be happening? How could her worst nightmares be coming true?

"Get. Out."

Hardly able to breathe, she backed slowly toward the outer door.

Sloan turned slightly to glance at her over his shoulder. "And don't worry. You won't have to prostitute yourself to me ever again. I'm long gone."

The words hurt, but what she saw in his eyes cemented the numbness spreading through her limbs.

She'd told herself all along, from the moment he'd seen her in the designer dress in Las Vegas, that she could do this as long as he looked at her a certain way—or any way except how men used to look at her mother. A mixture of lust, disgust and superiority. As long as that didn't show up on Sloan's face, she could put away all her insecurities and just be with him.

But now his eyes, those pale, electric blue eyes, were icy and cold, free of any emotion. His blank stare sliced through her, but she felt no pain.

She realized in that split second that as much as she wanted respectability and stability, had pushed herself to win Vivian's regard and respect, she couldn't care less about it in this moment. She didn't care that she'd lost everything.

All she cared about was Sloan.

But he didn't care about her. His willingness to walk away without a word, without listening to an explanation, told her everything she needed to know. That it had all been a lie.

Tears pushed into her eyes and she lowered her lids. She would not show vulnerability here, in this room that had seen the most sensual loving in her life. Now it was just a room. Cold and distant. She'd stay strong and protect herself, just as she'd been doing since she was a teenager.

The boxes once again caught her eye. Watching him pack up and leave, knowing he'd leave her behind without a twinge of regret, might just strip her of the stupor dulling everything— inside and out.

Ignoring him, she turned back to her own office. Luckily she hadn't put her purse away. The straps remained tightly clasped in one of her hands.

She wandered down the hallway as if in a trance. Nearing the turn, she heard Patrick's voice behind her. "Ziara, are you all right?"

She didn't acknowledge him, didn't even glance his way. For once she didn't care if it was her job to make things as easy as possible for her boss. Instinct said run, so she did—stepping into the elevator that opened before her like the doors to a haven.

Two days later Ziara lay motionless on her couch, staring up at the ceiling. The lights remained off, but she knew she would look a mess if anyone saw her. She'd managed to enter her bedroom only once and that had been to change out of her work clothes. She'd avoided it—and the memories of hours spent in her colorful bed with Sloan—since then.

She hadn't moved except to blink for two hours. Her mind whirled, reexamining the same questions over and over again. The one image that rose repeatedly was the look in Sloan's eyes when he'd glanced over his shoulder at her.

The blankness, so reminiscent of her life now.

She hurt too deeply to cry, to even move. So she held still and prayed it would all go away. She'd always been a doer, the type of person to take charge in a crisis, capable of handling most anything from her teen years on.

Now she simply endured.

Unable to face the office, she'd called the next day and spoken with Abigail, whose gentle voice had almost been her undoing. But then Vivian had come on the line.

"Though I'm disappointed, I completely understand how you could find yourself in this situation, Ziara," her mentor had said, her attitude far more subdued than in previous conversations. "Take a couple of days, but then we need you back in the office. The show is only seven days away and we can't afford for you to be absent longer than that. After the show, we'll talk."

Which probably meant: *I need you to get me through this event, but then you are fired.* Good or bad, she'd meet her obligations for the same reason she'd started working with Sloan—because she cared enough about Eternity Designs to see it succeed.

What she'd do after that, she didn't know.

Eighteen

Sloan stared at the blueprints for his newest reconstruction of an historic office building, but his thoughts turned again and again to the sketch of an imperial-style nightgown he knew was hiding underneath.

He should have moved on by now, but he couldn't. The show was tomorrow and he should be there, making sure everything ran smoothly, damn it.

His mind kept replaying Ziara's stiff back and shattered expression before she'd walked out of his office. Had he made a huge mistake? Had he let his pride mislead him from the truth?

She'd felt something for him. If he'd doubted it before that moment, he hadn't since. He didn't blame her for not saying it, for holding back. Not after seeing what she'd endured as a child.

He couldn't stop himself—he'd dug into Ziara's past the minute he'd returned to his old office. She'd come from a less than reputable family. Her mother had gotten pregnant with her very young—at seventeen. The same age at which Ziara had left home.

The father seemed to have been in the picture enough to

sign the birth certificate, but records indicated he'd left Macon not long after Ziara was born. His name hinted that he was the source of Ziara's exotic beauty—an Indian who had moved back to India five years ago after failing to make much of himself here in the U.S.

Vera's police record for prostitution started when Ziara was eight, with only a few arrests, but a quick conversation with an officer in Macon indicated she was well-known for her trade and generally left alone until some wife made a fuss. That same officer had told him Ziara left town as soon as she'd earned her GED, after years of being tormented by schoolmates who were well aware of her mother's profession.

But the information had only reinforced his decision to walk away. He didn't know where Vera Divan had gotten her information, or why she had confronted him that day—at least, not for sure. Suspicions lurked at the back of his mind, but honestly, the problem with Ziara meant more to him now than the business. He would not make Ziara pay any more than she already had for her upbringing. His physical relationship with her had given Vera the ammunition she'd needed to interfere in her daughter's life. What would stop her from doing it again? What if his suspicions were wrong?

Sloan sighed, running rough hands through his hair. It sucked when you realized you were in love with someone as you walked away from them.

Looking back, he could see that Ziara was ashamed, not just of her past, but of the things her mother did for money. So she'd run as far in the other direction as she could.

The buzz of the doorbell pulled Sloan's thoughts away from the scenarios swirling through his brain. Striding the length of the house, he jerked the door open. "Yes?"

"Don't have to be so short about it, Sloan."

Frowning at Patrick, whose incessant phone calls had about driven him crazy, he turned away without a word.

"Love you, too, jackass," his friend called out behind him. He didn't let Sloan's reticence stop him from coming in and making himself at home.

"What are you doing here?"

"Well, since you stopped answering my calls, what choice did I have?"

"You could have just stopped calling me. Or gone home. After all, you don't have a job here anymore."

"And let you throw away something you've worked damn hard for? Not a chance." Patrick just kept on coming. "And I do have a job, thanks to a certain someone whose name you forbid me to say."

"What happened?"

"If you wanted to know, you should have answered my phone calls."

Sloan glared, torn between curiosity and the pain of hearing her name. Patrick simply stood there with a smirk on his face, humming a few bars of "That's What Friends Are For." Infuriated, Sloan stomped through the house to the kitchen, jerking open the fridge to snag a Mountain Dew.

"I told you," Sloan said after returning and taking a long drink, "I have no interest in coming back. I'm certainly not wanted or needed there."

"According to who?"

"Vivian, for a start."

"Since when has her opinion ever counted for anything? In fact, it usually makes you do the opposite."

"Not this time."

"Why?" Patrick moved closer. "Sorry, bro, excuses are not gonna cut it."

"I told you what happened. She wouldn't even defend herself."

"Did you give her a chance or did you just railroad her with that overbearing attitude you get sometimes? Did you even tell her what you told me? What her mother said? I doubt she even knew what she was defending herself against. I told you that you were wrong…and this time, I can prove it."

"How?"

"Ziara went to bat for you—against Vivian."

Something tingled in Sloan's chest, but he ignored it. "What do you mean?"

"The lingerie line. Vivian wanted to cut it—and me—from the show. Ziara kept production moving until Vivian got wind of it, then she argued that it should stay. And so should I."

"How?" Sloan asked again, his throat tightening too much to get anything else out.

"The same argument you used, plus pointing out that a few choice tidbits have already been leaked to the press. Hints of a completely new direction for Eternity that has the RSVPs pouring in like water in a spring flood."

He was almost afraid of the answer. "Who alerted the press?"

"Not me. Not Robert or Anthony, who were surprisingly supportive of her arguments, by the way."

"Yeah?"

Patrick nodded. "So I'm guessing that only leaves one choice. Unless you did it yourself?"

"No way." Sloan's hands lifted in a hands-off gesture. "I want nothing to do with this show. Nothing."

Patrick leaned closer, his knowing look pinning Sloan where he stood. "You sure? You haven't been looking at any designs, thinking about fabric or drape or weight?" He wiggled his eyebrows. "It's very sexy when a woman comes to her man's defense."

"I'm not her man."

"Deep down, you know Ziara had nothing to do with her mother's blackmail threat. Time to admit you were wrong."

Sloan turned to face the bay window, staring out over his wooded backyard. "What if I'm not?"

"Don't you want to be?"

"Yes," Sloan said. It was harder to admit than he'd thought it would be, but it was the truth. He wanted Ziara to be innocent; he wanted that shattered look on her face to be real—not some kind of act that she'd learned from her conniving mother.

"Then don't worry about it. I, personally, am pinning my money on Vivian," Patrick said, his voice deepening in disgust.

"But I have no proof."

"And you'll never get it brooding around your house. Get back in the game, you coward."

Sloan would never have tolerated it from anyone else, but from Patrick, he knew those words were the honest truth. It was time to put his protective armor aside, face the fact that he loved Ziara and give her a chance to prove her innocence.

"Vivian will fire Ziara after this," Sloan said. "She's never tolerated me being a part of anything."

Patrick nodded. "With or without you, I think that's already her plan."

When Ziara arrived at the fashion show venue, it was a scene of organized chaos. Watching for one last quiet moment, an achy sadness spread through her. After tonight, her job at Eternity Designs would be done and she'd be on her own again. The loneliness had started creeping in earlier this week, an extension of Sloan's absence.

Spotting Patrick, she eagerly walked down the aisle, anxious not to be alone with her thoughts.

"It's beautiful," she breathed, staring at the simulated 1930s nightclub, elegant in its classic simplicity, sexy with silver and black details. The colors of the dresses and lingerie would look amazing against that backdrop. Peeking from a side wing, as if it had just dropped off guests at the show, was a 1930s silver Rolls-Royce classic car.

"Isn't it, doll?" Patrick said. "And the background changes colors." He paused. "But I guess you already knew that."

"Yes, I did," she said with a sad smile as she remembered the day she and Sloan had picked it out, together. Tucking away the pain, she turned all business. "Time to get ready for opening night, huh?"

By early evening she was a weird combination of tired and wired, with a long night still ahead of them. She didn't attend the preshow hors d'oeuvres, but she watched the crowd arrive for the event. Vivian was in her element, glimmering in a golden lace overlay gown as she smiled and conversed with members of Atlanta's elite.

No, not just Atlanta's, or even Georgia's. Ziara recognized a few of the surrounding states' political figures, not to mention the buyers for their usual venues and a few New York buyers, too.

Her heart fluttered, her stomach tightening like a fist. So much rode on this event for Eternity Designs and Sloan, even though he didn't seem to care anymore. Surely all the hard work and turmoil would be worthwhile.

Surely her heartache wouldn't be for nothing.

Ziara took her gown backstage to change. It was the same dress Patrick had sent her to wear for his party, topped with a sheer wrap in deference to the cooler fall nights.

Coming out of the dressing room, she had to walk through the space they'd set aside to prep the models. It was already filling up with half-naked women who had Ziara looking askance. A smile tugged at her mouth as she came across Patrick, kneeling behind a scantily clad model wearing a gorgeous burnt-orange negligee." Isn't this how we met?"

He grinned up at her before finishing the last few stitches. Then he stood. "I'm done, Jennifer. Thanks." He turned to her as the model walked away. "You look stunning in that dress, Ziara."

"Thank you. The designer did an incredible job." She leaned over to brush a kiss on his cheek, only to jump when someone said, "What's this?"

Hearing Sloan's voice was a little surreal. Turning, she was at a loss for words as she faced those bright blue eyes.

Patrick spoke from behind her. "You sure know how to make an entrance, buddy."

Sloan's grin made her heart ache, but she couldn't stop looking. The cool, calm facade she'd rebuilt over the past week cracked under his stare.

"Why…why are you here, Sloan?" she asked, clearing her throat in an attempt to get the words out.

"I'd like to know that myself." Vivian's voice drew their

gazes as she stormed through the curtain. "I was told you had arrived, but I have no idea for what purpose." Her eyes swept over their little group before resting back on her stepson. "I'm waiting, Sloan."

Ziara felt herself take a step back, afraid of the coming storm. Fights between Sloan and Vivian were notoriously intense, and she really wasn't up to enduring one at the moment.

"Then you'll be waiting a long time, Vivian," Sloan said. "I don't answer to you. Nor do I need an invite to my own show."

Vivian sputtered, "It's not your show."

"Oh, it is. Unless you'd like me to confiscate every dress, every item I had a hand in creating, carrying them to my car right through the front door. Your guests would love that, and we'd certainly make the society pages. And you'd still have a few left to show, I guess." The charming grin that got Ziara every time made an appearance. "Just not the best ones."

"You wouldn't dare." His charm was definitely lost on Vivian.

"Oh, I would. I assure you." He rubbed those incredibly skilled hands together. "I'm back in."

Nineteen

"Excuse me?" The high-pitched squeal in her voice would have mortified Vivian if she'd been more aware of it.

"You heard me," Sloan said, enjoying Vivian's distress. His eyes remained on her, but his senses were searching out Ziara's reactions to his presence. Now, just like the first time, she distracted him. Everything that made him a man told him to end this argument so he could sweep her away to a back room somewhere. But it was too soon for that.

Too much unfinished business between them.

"Oh no, Sloan. You left of your own accord," Vivian said.

"I prefer to think of it as a vacation."

The frustration reddening her face wasn't pretty. "That's simply semantics. It won't hold up in court."

"Wanna bet? Besides, I'm pretty sure Patrick will testify that I've been in touch with him over the past few days about final details. In my opinion, that counts." Thank goodness for Patrick's pestering. "This is simply a courtesy notice. I'll see you on the stage later." With a wink at his friend and Ziara, he turned toward the stage exit.

"So you decided you believed the little slut after all? What did she do, beg you to take her back?"

Sloan halted in midstride. He heard Ziara's gasp behind him, but forced himself to focus on Vivian alone. If she wanted to do this out in the open, let her hang herself with her own rope.

She kept right on talking. "I didn't count on that idealistic streak of your father's running through you as well, so the sexual harassment angle was definitely the way to go. I guess love didn't mean much in the face of prosecution."

Sloan pivoted slowly, his body tensing into standard negotiation mode. He'd thought the hardest part of regaining his father's company would be bluffing his way back into the deal. He'd never imagined Vivian would admit to having met Vera Divan first.

Ziara stood directly in his line of vision, her eyes trained on Vivian. Her olive skin now held a pale undertone and her gaze was hazy, unfocused, as she absorbed a blow he should have protected her from.

Patrick stepped in this time. "How did you even get Vera Divan to approach Sloan?"

"People like that will do anything for money, unlike us." Vivian kept speaking, digging the hole deeper and deeper. "She's just the daughter of a whore, Sloan. Or are you finally ready to sink to their level? Your mother's lower-class roots making themselves known."

That was all he needed. Stalking across the floor, he leaned in, dwarfing her with his size and his anger. His voice, when he spoke, was cool and deadly, but Vivian didn't seem to notice. "Actually I'm back here because my father's idealism runs strong through my veins. I want his dream to grow and thrive, not become some kind of shrine to the marriage you wanted but could never have. You always knew you were second-best, which is why you turned my father against me."

"You were simply a reminder of *her,* all free spirit and no responsibilities. The memories are what kept him from moving forward. He could have loved me just as much, given time."

"But there just wasn't enough time for you to mold him

into what you wanted, was there?" Sloan asked, his breath speeding up as he remembered the pain of the wedge Vivian drove between them. "As for Ziara, watch how you speak about her," he said. "She's not the daughter of a whore. She's a strong woman, who inspires me to be the person my father wanted me to be. She's worked hard to get where she is. She chose respectability when she could have given up, followed in her mother's footsteps. That's an example of refinement you'll never understand."

Vivian's eyes widened, fear creeping in at the edges.

Digging deep, Sloan remembered that last special moment with his father—his memories of following the taller man as he pushed through the crowd with sure steps. Sloan forged ahead. "I value traditions just as much as my father did, and he was right about one thing—you and I can't work together. So I think it would be best if you retire when Abigail does. I would hate for word to leak out about your shady dealings with Ziara's mother."

"You couldn't do that without telling people about Ziara's past."

"Who gives a damn? I certainly don't care what people think. She's not her mother—in any way. And anyone who dare speaks even her name wrong will have to deal with me. Personally."

This time Sloan's exit was straight and true. He walked out with a new connection to his father and a woman he still needed to seduce—this time into happily ever after.

Ziara glanced down at her hands, the slight vibration a little surprising. She wasn't sure if it was from witnessing the confrontation between Sloan and Vivian, or the sheer shock from seeing him again. In her heart, she knew he was only here for the business, for his father's memory. His surprising defense of her made her wish for something else, for something more personal, more private.

As she watched the glamorous throng being urged to their seats, she knew it wouldn't happen. Now that the truth was out, she'd never fit into this world. Vivian would make sure of that. And Sloan would never want to fit into hers.

As everyone settled and the lights dimmed, Ziara took a deep breath. This was it. The moment of truth. The reception of these lines would make or break Eternity Designs.

Things went well from the beginning. Guests oohed and aahed in all the right places as the wedding gowns graced the spotlight. The tightness coiled deep inside Ziara loosened as the first model for the transitional lingerie line made her entrance. Her dark coloring set off the white, slim-fitting gown against the now-pale pink backdrop.

As the emcee explained the nature of the material and the gown's function, Ziara heard whispers, and flashbulbs exploded. Just at that moment one of the runners stuck his head around the side door and motioned for Ziara.

As she approached, he whispered, "Miss Ziara, we need you."

Duty called.

Ziara and Patrick arrived back in the side wing just as Sloan started his speech. Tears in need of release ached in Ziara's throat. But she'd gotten through tonight, just as she would get through whatever lay ahead. Even if it meant starting over somewhere else.

Drinking in Sloan's confident, cocky grin as he addressed the crowd, she wished her future would keep her with Sloan.

Patrick left her side to join the other designers as Sloan introduced them. They looked like a melting pot of styles side by side, but the combination had been wildly successful. The standing ovation was proof positive.

Standing alone in the wings, Ziara's heart warmed with gratitude. Sloan had attained success, just as he deserved. He'd been right and she and Vivian had been wrong. In the end he'd saved the company they all loved.

Catching a change in Sloan's voice drew her focus back to him.

"There's one other person I must thank for making tonight

the success it is. Not only did she work tirelessly behind the scenes, she played mediator, organizer and even stagehand."

Ziara's heart thumped so loudly Sloan's next words were almost blocked out. "But most importantly, she served as the inspiration behind some of my new lingerie pieces. She taught me a very important lesson—the most amazing thing you can do in life is to be true to yourself. Not what people want you to be, the mold they shove you into, but to be what you want in life. That's the greatest challenge. She encouraged me to create some of the designs you saw tonight, and it's one of the most fulfilling things I've ever done. I hope my father would be proud."

He turned, staring straight at the spot where she trembled backstage. Gooseflesh prickled her bare arms as she listened.

"Please welcome Ziara Divan, my executive assistant at Eternity Designs."

When his hand extended toward her, she knew he meant for her to join him. Her mind was numb, yet she forced one leaden foot in front of another. As she stepped from the shadows out into the bright lights and applause, her mind came alive, racing with a dozen questions.

She ignored them, intent on reaching Sloan's side to slip her shaking hand into his outstretched one. Leaning down, he buried his head once again in the hair near her ear. "I love you, Ziara."

She shook her head, pulling back to stare with wonder into those glittering blue eyes. "What about—" she began in fear.

Sloan silenced her with one warm finger against her lips.

She heard the crowd erupt into applause, but she could only lose herself in Sloan's hot gaze and hope the fears would disappear like mist under the heat of his desire.

Later that night, long after the last guest was gone and the last dress packed away, Sloan found himself enjoying a very different kind of show in the privacy of his luxurious bathroom.

"Sloan, I really can't do this."

"Ziara, look at me." Sloan gently cupped her chin, guiding it up so she could watch the two of them in the full-length mirror. He knew she didn't want to see herself, but he wasn't going to let her hide. His gaze devoured her sensuous curves in the coppery silk. He probably shouldn't push her tonight, after everything she'd been through at the show, but part of him needed her to see the truth.

When he'd said she had been the inspiration for his lingerie pieces, he hadn't been lying. But this particular piece had been created for her—and him—alone. Like layered veils of transparent copper, burnt-orange, pale yellow and gold, the floor-length sheath both covered and revealed the curves of her body. Tempting him with her exotic beauty, showcasing the woman she was meant to be.

"Are you your mother?"

Her sharp intake of breath threatened to strain the zipper, but he wasn't backing down.

"Answer me."

"No, not even a little bit," she said, her assurance translating to her body. Her shoulders straightened. Her tension dissolved.

"Are you a beautiful woman who deserves to wear pretty things? Who wants to see how strong and sexy she is?"

Swallowing hard, her constrained voice came out a whisper. "Yes."

"Then wear this. For me."

Sloan let his eyes wander down her reflection. Luscious mounds of plump flesh overflowed the cups. While the effect wasn't quite pornographic, his body responded by tightening immediately, hard and throbbing. He'd fantasized about Ziara in various pieces of the lingerie he'd designed, but they hadn't gotten around to her wearing any for him. The reality was more spectacular than he'd imagined.

Unable to wait any longer, he did the one thing he'd been dying to since he'd seen her backstage earlier that evening—covered her lips with his own.

She pulled back way too soon. "Please understand, I didn't do this for any other reason—" He could almost hear her throat close, hear the fear she hid inside.

He knew of only one way to convince her of his love, to prove how much she deserved to be cherished and respected. That he wanted to be with her for an entire lifetime. Only one way to break through her barriers and convince the woman within.

He eased his hands up her back. When he buried his hands in her hair, pins clattered to the tile floor. He ran his fingers through the thick silk, searching for any remaining pins, then massaged her scalp until she relaxed, tension easing from her muscles. She melted against him. Tipping her face up to meet his, he was surprised to find silent tears trailing down her cheeks.

"Oh, baby, don't cry," he murmured.

"I'm not," she insisted. Swiping a hand at her cheeks, she stared at the moisture on her fingers in disbelief. He barely caught her whisper. "I've never cried, not since I was fourteen years old. Until I met you."

He guided her gaze up to meet his with a finger under her chin. "There's no need to, because I believe you. I believe *in* you."

A hopeful expression lit her darkened eyes just as her legs gave out. He clasped her to him, picking her up and striding down the passageway toward his bedroom.

He laid her on the bed, then explored her slowly, tracing every tantalizing curve through the soft fabric—her shoulders, neck, hips, calves, then back up to her stomach and breasts. Every hitch of her breath, every tremble in her limbs drew him closer, tightening the connection that bound them together— mind, body and soul.

"I can't believe how this feels," she whispered. "How you feel. I never want it to end."

"Me, either," he said before burying his face between her breasts. The round, soft weights tempted him, and were almost as distracting as her dark, tight nipples. Pulling the cups aside, he savored them as much as he did her silent declaration. One day she'd be ready to speak her true feelings. Though he had a reputation for pushing to get what he wanted, this time he'd wait as long as necessary.

Finally, widening her thighs with his knee, he settled over her.

"Now I know why having you is so different for me," he said, lifting his gaze to watch her in the shadowed moonlight.

"Why?"

"Because I love you." With those words, he pressed inside her, savoring the slick heat of her body, the arch of her back and the gasp from her lips.

No other words were spoken between them as they strove for release, each giving as much as taking until the world exploded around them. Long moments later, Sloan opened his eyes to find Ziara staring at him. He quirked a lazy eyebrow, savoring their still-connected bodies. "What is it?"

Her words were hushed, as if in reverence to the intimate connection between them. "I can't believe you believe me, after all she must have said to you. How can you still love me?"

He thought for a moment, choosing his words with care. "I should have remembered that Vivian has her own kind of ruthlessness. I'd already started to suspect, but never dreamed she'd lose her cool enough to admit her involvement with your mother." He looked into eyes surrounded by the thickest lashes he'd ever seen. "I never dreamed I'd be stupid enough to fall for it."

Trailing his knuckle along the curve of her cheek, he said, "My father was right."

"About what?"

"He said loving my mother was pure magic."

He felt her awe in the softening of her body, the tiny smile that visited her lips. As he settled once more within her arms, his hand stroked along her thigh. His mind soaked in her presence. "I love you, Ziara," he said.

"I love you, too, Sloan."

Joy burst under his skin. He brushed a tender kiss along her temple, pausing a moment to savor her declaration. Tonight truly was magic. He'd fought for what he believed in and won. As he whispered erotic intentions in her ear, he vowed to turn their dreams into reality.

For all eternity.

* * * * *

#2251 STERN
The Westmorelands
Brenda Jackson
After his best friend's makeover, Stern Westmoreland suddenly wants her all for himself! Will he prove they can be much more than friends?

#2252 SOMETHING ABOUT THE BOSS...
Texas Cattleman's Club: The Missing Mogul
Yvonne Lindsay
Sophie suspects her new boss is involved in his business partner's disappearance, and she'll risk it all to uncover the truth...even if she has to seduce it out of him.

#2253 THE NANNY TRAP
Billionaires and Babies
Cat Schield
When his wife deserts their child, Blake hires the baby's surrogate mother as nanny—and desire unexpectedly ignites between them. But when the nanny reveals her secret, everything changes!

#2254 BRINGING HOME THE BACHELOR
The Bolton Brothers
Sarah M. Anderson
When the reformed "Wild" Bill Bolton finds himself as the prize at a charity bachelor auction, he has good girl Jenny thinking about taking a walk on the wild side!

#2255 CONVENIENTLY HIS PRINCESS
Married by Royal Decree
Olivia Gates
Aram's convenient bride turns out to be most inconvenient when he falls in love with her! But will Kanza believe in their love when the truth comes out?

#2256 A BUSINESS ENGAGEMENT
Duchess Diaries
Merline Lovelace
Sarah agreed to a fake engagement to save her sister, but the sexy business tycoon she's promised to—and the magic of Paris—make it all too real!

You can find more information on upcoming Harlequin® titles, free excerpts and more at www.Harlequin.com.

HDCNM0813

REQUEST YOUR FREE BOOKS!
2 FREE NOVELS PLUS 2 FREE GIFTS!

⊕HARLEQUIN®

Desire

ALWAYS POWERFUL, PASSIONATE AND PROVOCATIVE

YES! Please send me 2 FREE Harlequin Desire® novels and my 2 FREE gifts (gifts are worth about $10). After receiving them, if I don't wish to receive any more books, I can return the shipping statement marked "cancel." If I don't cancel, I will receive 6 brand-new novels every month and be billed just $4.55 per book in the U.S. or $4.99 per book in Canada. That's a savings of at least 13% off the cover price! It's quite a bargain! Shipping and handling is just 50¢ per book in the U.S. and 75¢ per book in Canada.* I understand that accepting the 2 free books and gifts places me under no obligation to buy anything. I can always return a shipment and cancel at any time. Even if I never buy another book, the two free books and gifts are mine to keep forever.

225/326 HDN F4ZC

Name _____ (PLEASE PRINT) _____

Address _____ Apt. # _____

City _____ State/Prov. _____ Zip/Postal Code _____

Signature (if under 18, a parent or guardian must sign)

Mail to the Harlequin® Reader Service:

IN U.S.A.: P.O. Box 1867, Buffalo, NY 14240-1867
IN CANADA: P.O. Box 609, Fort Erie, Ontario L2A 5X3

**Want to try two free books from another line?
Call 1-800-873-8635 or visit www.ReaderService.com.**

* Terms and prices subject to change without notice. Prices do not include applicable taxes. Sales tax applicable in N.Y. Canadian residents will be charged applicable taxes. Offer not valid in Quebec. This offer is limited to one order per household. Not valid for current subscribers to Harlequin Desire books. All orders subject to credit approval. Credit or debit balances in a customer's account(s) may be offset by any other outstanding balance owed by or to the customer. Please allow 4 to 6 weeks for delivery. Offer available while quantities last.

Your Privacy—The Harlequin® Reader Service is committed to protecting your privacy. Our Privacy Policy is available online at www.ReaderService.com or upon request from the Harlequin Reader Service.

We make a portion of our mailing list available to reputable third parties that offer products we believe may interest you. If you prefer that we not exchange your name with third parties, or if you wish to clarify or modify your communication preferences, please visit us at www.ReaderService.com/consumerchoice or write to us at Harlequin Reader Service Preference Service, P.O. Box 9062, Buffalo, NY 14269. Include your complete name and address.

HD13R

SPECIAL EXCERPT FROM

HARLEQUIN®

Desire

A sneak peek at

STERN, a *Westmoreland novel*

by New York Times *and* USA TODAY *bestselling author*

Brenda Jackson

Available September 2013.
Only from Harlequin® Desire!

As far as Stern was concerned, his best friend had lost her ever-loving mind. But he didn't say that. Instead, he asked, "What's his name?"

"You don't need to know that. Do you tell me the name of every woman you want?"

"This is different."

"Really? In what way?"

He wasn't sure, but he just knew that it was. "For you to even ask me, that means you're not ready for the kind of relationship you're going after."

JoJo threw her head back and laughed. "Stern, I'll be thirty next year. I'm beginning to think that most of the men in town wonder if I'm really a girl."

He studied her. There had never been any doubt in his mind that she was a girl. She had long lashes and eyes so dark they were the color of midnight. She had gorgeous legs, long and endless. But he knew he was one of the few men who'd ever seen them.

"You hide what a nice body you have," he finally said. He suddenly sat up straight in the rocker. "I have an idea.

What you need is a makeover."

"A makeover?"

"Yes, and then you need to go where your guy hangs out. In a dress that shows your legs, in a style that shows off your hair." He reached over and took the cap off her head. Lustrous dark brown hair tumbled to her shoulders. He smiled. "See, I like it already."

And he did. He was tempted to run his hands through it to feel the silky texture.

He leaned back and took another sip of his beer, wondering where such a tempting thought had come from. This was JoJo, for heaven's sake. His best friend. He should not be thinking about how silky her hair was.

He should not be bothered by the thought of men checking out JoJo, of men calling her for a date.

Suddenly, he was thinking that maybe a makeover wasn't such a great idea after all.

Will Stern help JoJo win her dream man?

STERN

by New York Times *and* USA TODAY
bestselling author Brenda Jackson

Available September 2013
Only from Harlequin® Desire!

HDEXP73264

THE NANNY TRAP

Cat Schield

*A Billionaires & Babies novel: Powerful men…
wrapped around their babies' little fingers*

When his wife deserts their child, Blake hires the baby's
surrogate mother as nanny—and desire unexpectedly
ignites between them. But when the nanny reveals her
secret, everything changes!

Look for *THE NANNY TRAP* next month by
Cat Schield, only from Harlequin® Desire.

Available wherever books and ebooks are sold.

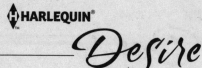

HARLEQUIN®
Desire
ALWAYS POWERFUL, PASSIONATE AND PROVOCATIVE.

CONVENIENTLY
HIS PRINCESS
Olivia Gates

**Part of the Married by Royal Decree series:
When the king commands, they say "I do!"**

Aram's convenient bride turns out to be most
inconvenient when he falls in love with her! But will
Kanza believe in their love when the truth comes out?

Find out next month in
CONVENIENTLY HIS PRINCESS by Olivia Gates,
only from Harlequin® Desire.

Available wherever books and ebooks are sold.

HD73268